'You feel it to

'Feel wh-what . . .

Darius gave a click of impatience, the gleam leaving his eyes.

'Oh, come *on*, Kitty,' he murmured. 'Don't deny what your body accepted minutes ago. Because you can't, can you? Your eyes are begging me to kiss you, aren't they?'

'N-no. They aren't,' she lied ineffectually.

He smiled. 'And do you know, I'm very tempted? *Very* tempted indeed!'

Sharon Kendrick was born in West London and has had *heaps* of jobs which include photography, nursing, driving an ambulance across the Australian desert and cooking her way around Europe in a converted double-decker bus! Without a doubt, writing is the best job she has ever had and when she's not dreaming up new heroes—some of which are based on her doctor husband!—she likes cooking, reading, theatre, drinking wine, listening to American west coast music and talking to her two children, Celia and Patrick.

PASSIONATE
FANTASY

BY
SHARON KENDRICK

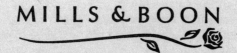

MILLS & BOON

To my mother and father with thanks and appreciation
for all their help and support over the years.

*MILLS & BOON and the Rose Device
are trademarks of the publisher.
Harlequin Mills & Boon Limited,
Eton House, 18-24 Paradise Road, Richmond, Surrey TW9 1SR
This edition published by arrangement with
Harlequin Enterprises B.V.*

© Sharon Kendrick 1995

ISBN 0 263 79079 7

*Set in Times Roman 11 on 12 pt.
01-9508-49372 C1*

Made and printed in Great Britain

CHAPTER ONE

I MUST be mad, thought Kitty as she knotted the ribbon in her hair before tying it in a bow. No, not just mad. Certifiable.

What *did* a girl wear for an interview with a world-famous film director?

She stared in the mirror again. Her ginger curls had gone totally wild after her shower, billowing into a mass of uncontrollable frizz. Very attractive! Just about the only thing she could do with it was to catch it back into a ponytail at the nape of her neck with a black velvet ribbon. Her pale, freckle-spattered skin was bare—she had discovered a long time ago that foundation was useless on a complexion which was basically two-tone! The eyelashes which surrounded her blue eyes were normally the same pale ginger-blonde as her hair, but every six weeks she dyed them black. It made her eyes look bigger, and it meant that she didn't have to mess around every morning applying mascara.

She had ummed and ahhed about what to wear. Mr Darius Speed would doubtless be used to women in up-market designer clothes, which was tough, since she didn't have any. Kitty had chosen instead a smart pair of cotton shorts in jade-green, with a matching silk scoop-necked T-shirt. There were a million colours you *couldn't* wear with ginger hair—

5

but fortunately green wasn't one of them. It would actually have been preferable to wear long sleeves to cover up her freckly arms, but the weather in Perth, Western Australia was sweltering and since Kitty had arrived two months ago she had had to abandon her much loved camouflage of jumpers and cardigans.

It was hard to believe that she was actually being interviewed for the job of cook to a man with the formidable reputation of Darius Speed. She would have thought that he'd have a top chef flown in from somewhere, but no—it seemed that he was interested in her, Kitty Goodman, with nothing to her name but a diploma from catering college.

What Mr Speed *didn't* know was that Kitty was specifically interested in *him*, and not the job. Not romantically interested, of course, as so many women were—that was if you could believe half of what you read in the gossip-columns.

No, Kitty's interest was of a far more noble nature—she was on a mission for her new and very dear friend Caro—to prove to the world that the supposedly high-minded Mr Speed had ripped Caro off—had stolen the film-script which Caro had spent a lifetime working on, and was planning to use it under his own name!

It had astonished and horrified Kitty to discover just how devious she could be. She had planned this interview with the film-maker with the precision of a military campaign. She had applied to him first in a letter, stating her qualifications and references. What had seemed like ages had passed, until she had been certain that she was out of the running—and then a well-spoken man had rung her up out of the blue to arrange an interview time.

'Are you free tomorrow evening?' the voice had asked.

She had remembered Caro showing her the newspaper clipping which had pictured a girl draped round the film director's neck like a boa-constrictor. 'Tomorrow *evening*, Mr Speed?' she had enquired frostily.

'I'm not,' an amused-sounding voice had said, 'Darius Speed. I'm Simon Parker—his secretary.'

'It seems rather an—odd—time for an interview,' Kitty had ventured.

The voice had sounded even more amused. 'Not so much odd as unusual. He's an unusual man. And besides, he's out doing research during the day.'

'Oh.'

'So are you available or not?'

It had struck Kitty that he could have chosen a word with slightly less awkward connotations than 'available', in the light of what Caro had told her about Darius Speed's reputation with the fairer sex, and she couldn't help feeling a little shiver of apprehension, half tempted to tell him no. But then she had thought about what she had promised Caro. 'Yes,' she had said, forcing a note of enthusiasm into her voice. 'I'm free.'

'Good. Can you meet him in Barbary's restaurant at eight? Oh, and don't eat first.'

A meeting in a restaurant. At night. Don't eat first. Kitty's face, she hoped, hid her misgivings as she paid her cab fare and walked into the fashionable and already crowded restaurant at five minutes before the appointed time.

'Mr Speed, please,' she said to the *maître d'*.

He gave her an expansive smile. 'Mr Speed hasn't arrived, madam. If you would like me to show you to your table?'

She followed him across the room to a table which was suitably central for an important customer, yet far enough away from other tables to prevent any conversation being overheard.

'Would madam like a drink?'

'Just a mineral water, please,' she said instantly, vowing that alcohol wouldn't cloud her senses. 'Sparkling.'

The drink was produced immediately in a long crystal glass packed with ice, with a piece of lime floating decorously on the surface, and Kitty had just started sipping it when there was the momentary lull which, she knew, heralded the arrival of Somebody Very Important, and the man whose photograph she had seen in the newspaper appeared in the doorway.

Darius Speed.

He looked straight across the restaurant, at the table at which she was sitting, and their eyes met. He stood very still for a moment, and stared hard at her. His own face was stern, although he said something to the *maître d'* which produced a wide smile.

Wow! was her first thoroughly instinctive thought. In the photograph he had looked devastating, but in the flesh he was something else! He had to be the most delectable man she had ever,

ever set eyes on, and then she reminded herself what kind of man he was, and immediately felt appalled at herself.

He began to walk towards her, full of both grace and power, and Kitty watched him approach, suddenly exceedingly nervous of what she was intending to do. She was intending to infiltrate the house of this man, to gain his trust, and then coolly to rob him. And while that was OK in theory, the reality of such an intimidating opponent quite unnerved her.

He was so much *bigger* than she had imagined—well over six feet—and his shoulders were distinctly and disturbingly broad. His hair was as dark as the night, unmarred by any trace of grey. And as he came closer to the table she could see that his eyes were the light, mercurial colour of quicksilver—grey one minute, silver the next.

He wore a suit in some dark grey material which fell loosely about the powerful frame, yet hinted at the strength which lay beneath, but there all conventionality ended because beneath the suit he was tieless, wearing a shirt of black silk—the hard inky colour somehow at odds with the softness of the material, as the penetrating look in his eyes was curiously at odds with the polite half-smile he gave her as he extended his hand.

'Miss Goodman? No, don't get up—I'm Darius Speed.'

She took the hand he offered, felt it give hers the most cursory of firm squeezes, before he sat down opposite her, his eyes questioning as he waited for her to speak.

'Good evening, Mr Speed.' Stop sounding like a mouse speaking to a lion, she told herself firmly.

'Darius,' he corrected shortly. 'And you're Kitty?'

She nodded, taking her courage in both hands. 'I am.'

The grey eyes flicked over her face, briefly taking in the well-pressed but fairly unremarkable outfit she wore. 'You don't,' he said, the deep voice holding the faintest undercurrent of warning—or was that just in her guilty imagination—'look in the least bit like a cook.'

Her instinct was to counter-attack, but she wanted the job, so she forced herself to be pleasant. From everything that Caro had told her, she already despised this man, but he wasn't going to discover that. Not for a little while, anyway. 'Whereas you,' she smiled, 'look exactly like a film director.'

There was an almost imperceptible tensing of his facial muscles. 'You've heard of me, then?'

'Naturally,' she concurred. 'I'm applying to work for you, aren't I?'

Grey eyes narrowed instantly. 'But the job description said only that the successful applicant would be working for a businessman. I don't remember specifying which business.'

'Well, I recognised you as soon as you walked into the restaurant,' she amended hastily. 'From your photo in the paper.'

He leaned back a little. 'Did you?' he enquired lazily, and Kitty got a strange and vivid impression that he would easily be able to differentiate be-

tween truth and fiction. She had better be careful.
'Well, that makes a refreshing change,' he said.

'What do you mean?'

He shrugged, the movement causing a dark
tendril of hair to stray on to his high and faintly
tanned forehead. 'You have no idea,' he said, 'how
many young women believe that it will elicit my
lasting and unswerving dedication if they play-act—
usually badly—failing to recognise me. The implication being, I imagine, that I will respect a woman
far more if she likes me for being just me, rather
than for the attraction of my fame and my money.'

Kitty remembered one of her mother's lessons.
She counted to ten, but as she did so she began to
savour putting into action her plan to extricate the
script from this intolerably arrogant man! 'Dear
me,' she said placatingly. 'How difficult relationships can be—as I know to my cost! You don't
appear to have had very much luck either.'

It was the gentlest of put-downs. Obviously *not*
what he was expecting her to say. He should have
had the grace to look abashed.

He didn't.

'You don't look like a chef,' he observed again.

'Don't I?' She gave a serene smile. 'You would
have preferred the stereotype, perhaps? A good ten
pounds overweight, checked trousers, a white jacket
with tall matching hat? Perhaps the tip of my nose
covered in flour would have added the final convincing touch?'

There was the faintest smile, before the handsome
face resumed a mocking mask. 'Something like
that,' he said softly.

She looked straight into the flashing silver eyes. Oh, that voice, she thought reluctantly. Had she ever heard a voice like that before? Never. It sounded like chocolate and honey. Like music played by some deep, sexy instrument. With the faintest of underlying drawls which made it especially distinctive. She sighed. Why couldn't he have looked like the back end of a bus? Much easier, surely, to deceive someone who didn't bring you out in goose-bumps all over.

The silver-grey eyes were unwavering. 'Now,' he said crisply. 'Before we go any further, I have to tell you that I'm looking for a chef and not an actress.'

She stared at him uncomprehendingly. 'What do you mean?' she asked slowly.

'Think about it.'

Comprehension slowly dawned. 'You think—that I'm really an actress? That my applying for the job of cook is simply a ploy to get to meet you?'

'You've got it in one,' he murmured.

Of all the *insufferable* arrogance! Stealing from this man was going to be pure, undiluted joy! 'You've seen my certificates,' she said coldly. 'You must know I'm bona fide.'

'Oh, yes—I've seen them.' He laughed then, a sort of bitter, empty laugh. 'But you'd be surprised,' he drawled, 'just how many women try it on. The whole world, it seems, wants to break into the movie business. I ring out for pizza—the girl who delivers it belts out a number from last year's musical. I go shopping, and the woman selling me the sweater asks can she visit me on set to audition.

Not just women, either. I take a bus and the driver gives me a rendition of Macbeth's soliloquy. Yes——' he must have seen her disbelieving expression '—bus. I don't travel exclusively by limousine. If I cut myself off from real life, then I can't make real films.'

What a cynic! Kitty drew a deep breath. 'Listen to me,' she told him. 'I cannot recite poetry or dance to save my life. When I start to sing, people leave the room in droves. I have no desire in the world to become an actress. Cooking is what I do best, and I enjoy it. At the moment I'm temping—mostly waitress work—handing out microwaved food with stupid names to people who don't need it. I answered your advertisement because I want to go back to cooking, which is why I'm here, though heaven knows—a restaurant seems a bizarre place in which to conduct an interview——'

'You think so?' Unexpectedly he gave a wolfish grin and handed her one of the leather-bound menus which the *maître d'* had placed silently on the table in front of him during their little discourse, as though he hadn't dared to interrupt. 'I can't think of a better place to interview someone who works with food.'

'Oh, I see.' She nodded in comprehension as she took the menu and scanned it. 'This is to be trial by bread and butter, is it? I'll be pilloried if I commit a crime so heinous as ordering strawberries out of season, or liberally sprinkling my food with pepper and salt without having tasted it first...?' She looked up to find that his eyes were fixed with amusement on her face. It was there for a moment, and then it was gone, and, in the few seconds that it took, her heart-rate underwent an alarming acceleration.

'Do you always have an answer for everything?' he mused.

She stared down at the menu, the handwritten italic script just meaningless hieroglyphics to her confused eyes. No, she didn't. This verbal jousting had been sparked by him. *Him*. And admit it, she thought, you *enjoyed* sparring with him. You liked the fact that you were able to make him smile.

'She retreats,' he commented. 'Wondering whether she has taken one step too far.'

If it weren't for Caro, she'd be taking more than one step, she fumed silently. She'd be taking several, right out of here, and away from Darius Speed with his alarming attraction.

'What should I have?' he queried casually. 'What can a restaurant best be judged on?'

It was a relief to be able to concentrate on something other than what a hunk hc was. Her special field. 'Something fresh,' she replied promptly, 'which can't be successfully reheated. Here I would try the eggs Florentine—poached eggs, béarnaise sauce and spinach—a simple dish which is heaven if it's done properly, hell if it's not.'

He nodded. 'If——'

'Mr Speed...'

They both looked up. A woman, who looked as though she had been poured into a black satin dress, stood looking down at them. The hair which tumbled artfully over her shoulders was blonde, but with the falsely honeyed hue of bottled peroxide.

He raised dark eyebrows. 'Yes?' he enquired non-committally.

'*Mr* Speed,' she gushed, 'I've been a fan of yours for *so* long. I *loved* your last film, and——'

'There's a problem, Mr Speed?' It was the professional voice of the *Maître d'*.

'No problem,' he came back implacably. 'What can I do for you, Miss...?'

'Arnold,' she gushed. 'Ffyona Arnold—that's with two fs and a y. Could I have your—autograph?' She batted sooty lashes and gave a little-girl smile. '*Please*?'

'Sure.'

Kitty thought she detected a faint sigh as he took a gold fountain-pen from the pocket of his jacket and accepted the card which Ffyona Arnold offered.

Was this what it was like, then—fame? wondered Kitty. That elusive twentieth-century symbol of success, chased by so many and given to so few. Was this all it was? Total strangers disturbing you in restaurants, transparent in their eagerness for something more than a mere signature?

'What would you like me to write?' he asked politely.

Ffyona Arnold gave another coquettish smile. 'How about the chance to show you what I can do—acting-wise, I mean?' She giggled hopefully, then must have seen the barely concealed look of boredom on his face. 'Your phone number would do,' she gushed.

Good heavens, thought Kitty, the woman must have the skin of a rhinoceros not to have picked up the negative vibes which were shimmering across the table from where the film-maker sat.

'Sorry.' He negated her request with a tone of chilly indifference, signing his name instead with a sweepingly confident flourish, and handed the card back with a polite gesture of dismissal.

After the disappointed woman had been firmly led away by the *Maître d'*, he turned back to Kitty, and she could see the mild expression of distaste which curled his lips. Was that all for her benefit? she wondered. If he hadn't been interviewing, would he have taken the woman up on her blatant offer? Taken her back to his house for a night of decadence?

He gestured towards her now empty glass. 'Something stronger?' he enquired. 'Some wine perhaps?'

'No, thank you. Just mineral water,' she said, much too quickly, and, suddenly nervous, knocked over the small crystal salt-cellar by her hand, and it tipped on to its side, salt spilling out in a small pile, a snowy little mountain growing on the crisp damask of the tablecloth.

There was a short silence while a waiter rushed over, brushed up the residue and replaced the salt-cellar, and she couldn't miss the searching look Darius Speed gave her, the eyes narrowed as if he hadn't expected clumsiness from her; and normally he would have been right. Normally.

'Tell my why you applied for this job,' he said, a cool impartiality making the deep voice devoid of any emotion.

He mustn't suspect, she thought desperately. He mustn't.

'You pay well,' she said, and she saw him give a small nod as though he understood the language of hard currency very well. 'Enough for me to save up and see the rest of Australia.'

'You could have done that in one of the established restaurants—of which Perth has many—some of them with world-class reputations. And you could have learnt from one of the master chefs.'

She shook her head. 'I'd have ended up chopping garlic in one corner of the kitchen. Working on my own gives me professional autonomy—and I like that.'

'Do you?' He nodded, and continued to subject her to that steady, cool stare, his eyes now the colour of pewter, shadowed by thick, dark lashes. 'And is there anything you'd care to ask me— Kitty?'

Don't seem too eager. He wouldn't give the job to just anyone. This kind of man would value someone only if she valued herself. She took a sip of iced mineral water, returning his cool stare with one of her own. 'I'm surprised that you need a full-time chef. Being a single man, that is.'

'You assume that I'm single, then? Been reading the papers again?'

'Not at all,' she shot back. 'I made the assumption because, if you were married, then I would certainly have expected your wife to take part in the choice of chef.'

'Because cooking is a woman's province, perhaps?'

'Because of equality within the relationship,' she countered. 'And some of the world's greatest chefs are men, as I'm sure you know.'

'Indeed. Very generously conceded, Kitty. And you're right—I *am* single.' He smiled, and sipped his own mineral water. 'I'm writing a screenplay,' he said, 'as well as auditioning for a film I'll be making, starting in January. I'm also researching a documentary on Rottnest Island, which the Western Australian government has asked me to make. So there will be film people in and out of the house. I keep very odd hours, because when I work I work. I also entertain people from all over the world, and I prefer to do that at home. In restaurants, there are often...' His eyes shot over to the other side of the room, where Ffyona Arnold was sitting, ignoring her dining companion and gazing at Darius. When she saw him look over, she gave him a hopeful smile, but he did not return it.

'There are distractions,' he continued surprisingly, and Kitty knew a moment's confusion. He sounded as if he disapproved of the kind of 'distraction' that Ffyona Arnold represented—and yet surely, according to what Caro had told her, he would be pleased to meet a woman who would jump into bed for less than the price of dinner?

'Sometimes I may fly in at some unearthly hour,' he went on, 'and require you to put a meal together for me, so the job needs a live-in cook. Does that bother you?'

The look was penetrating. She gave a nervous swallow. 'Not at all. It'll save rent.'

Another twist of the mouth. 'You aren't worried about giving up your independence?'

'I don't know anyone in Perth, really,' she lied, and then, because she was afraid that she would blush and give herself away, she moved away from that particular subject. 'The only thing I feel you ought to know is that I can't guarantee that I'll stay with you for any more than a year.' Or more than a week, if she could get the script by then! 'Would that matter to you?'

He didn't smile. 'It would suit me perfectly. If I may be frank—by that time you'll probably have begun to irritate me, and I you. I have a very low boredom threshold.' He ignored her shocked intake of breath at his blatant rudeness. 'The job's yours, Kitty. Do you want it?'

Her skin beneath the jade silk T-shirt felt suddenly shivery, even though the temperature in the restaurant was equable. The tips of her breasts tingled strangely, as if her reflexes were instinctively telling her to steer clear. For one moment she was tempted just to push her chair back and walk out through that door, not caring what he or the other diners thought. But then a vision of Caro imposed itself on her mind. Dear, kind Caro. Caro on the brink of tears. Her life's work pirated by a man with no scruples.

She met the spectacular grey stare, and blinked, as if afraid that those intelligent eyes had been perceptive enough to understand her silent tussle. 'I'd be pleased to accept,' she said quietly.

'Good.' He gave a nod in the direction of the back of the restaurant, and Kitty saw a tall, slim man with brown hair rise from a discreet corner table and come towards their own.

'This is Simon,' said Darius Speed, 'my secretary. I believe you've already spoken. He will fill you in on all the details of your employment over dinner. Afterwards he will arrange for one of my cars to drop you at your home. Please feel free to order what you want. I have urgent business which I must attend to. Goodbye.' Another brief, firm contact as he shook her hand.

Kitty watched while he threaded his way through the restaurant, the attention of every single female in the room drawn to his tall, muscular physique.

And then Kitty saw something else. Did Simon notice, she wondered, or was it just her?

Seconds after Darius had disappeared into the plant-filled vestibule towards the exit, someone followed him. A woman encased in clinging black satin.

It was Ffyona Arnold, the autograph-hunter—she had left her companion to follow him—a rapacious look of anticipation all over her pretty, vacant face.

CHAPTER TWO

'CAN you take me to Dalkeith, please?' Kitty mentioned the name of the well-known Perth suburb to the taxi-driver.

He grinned. 'No worries. Whereabouts?'

'Jackland Parade.' She gave the name of the street, and the driver gave a long, low whistle.

'Millionaires' row?' he queried, and looked more closely at her as he handed in her two suitcases. 'Hit the big time, have you, love?'

Kitty flicked a thick ginger plait back over her shoulder. 'I've got a job there,' she told him.

'Lucky you,' he commented as he turned the key in the ignition.

Lucky? Her hands were cold and clammy. The way she felt at the moment, she was lucky she hadn't been committed to the nearest asylum to have her brain examined.

In the week since her successful interview with Darius Speed, Kitty had had time to reflect on the wisdom of attempting her madcap scheme. The man with the quicksilver grey eyes had disturbed her in more ways than one, but mostly it had been her recognition of his keen intelligence which had filled her with dread.

In the end it had been Caro who had talked away her fears, telling her that it would be simple. She could be in and out of there in a month, maybe a

21

week if she was lucky, with the film-script in her hand, and the eternal gratitude of her friend.

'But what if he suspects? Or, even worse, guesses why I'm there?'

Caro had shrugged in her happy-go-lucky way. 'How can he?' she had quizzed. 'You'll be in the kitchen most of the time—you'll hardly see him. He travels a lot, and while he's away you find out the combination of his safe.'

'How?' Kitty had demanded, ever practical.

Caro had smiled. 'You'll think of something.'

'Will I?'

'Of course you will! Honestly, Kitty, you'll be *fine*!'

But as the taxi waited outside electronic wrought-iron gates while a uniformed guard telephoned her name through to the house, Kitty felt like one of the Christians about to be fed to the lions. Even when they were given the all-clear, her nervousness showed no sign of abating.

They drove up to the impressive-looking two-storey white building. The gardens were extensive and beautiful, displaying much of the lush tropical flora which Kitty knew abounded in the state of Western Australia. She could see trees with bright exotic blossoms of red and mauve, standing out brilliantly against the clear blue of the sky.

She looked up at the house, her eyes registering its unpretentiousness—but, for all that, she knew that the property must be worth a cool half-million, at least.

But, to her surprise, the front door opened immediately, and it was not some uniformed minion who came out but Darius Speed himself, running lightly down the steps with all the grace and stamina of the natural athlete.

He was dressed in tennis whites: a short-sleeved T-shirt, slightly damp with sweat, and a pair of immaculate white shorts which came to mid-thigh, showing a long expanse of tanned and muscular leg. His hair was damp too, little tendrils dancing around the strong neck.

She stared up at him, momentarily transfixed. The sun was behind him—and his eyes were full of a clear, bright light which rivalled its brilliance. He looked, she thought, like the very antithesis of a blond Greek god—with his dark hair and his shadowed, mysterious face in repose.

But as he spoke her illusions fled. 'Hello, Kitty,' he said coolly. Then, as he saw her pull out her purse and begin to open it, he shook his head. 'I'll get this,' he said.

She watched, while pretending not to, as he walked towards the car. He had bent down, and was grinning at something the taxi-driver had said. Kitty gulped in unwilling admiration. At that moment he looked so carefree and so relaxed—the very picture of health and strength—a man at the very peak of his vitality. She began to wonder how a woman might feel to have those strong brown arms around her waist, to feel that lean, hard body pressed against——

'Such a pensive cook,' came a soft voice beside her, and she snapped out of her reverie in horror to find Darius at her side, a heavy suitcase carried in either hand with ease. 'And from the look on your face you were worrying about more than what equipment you're going to find in my kitchen?'

Hardly! And she certainly wasn't going to tell him what she had been thinking! She fixed him with her sweetest smile. 'I was imagining how you would react if my soufflé failed to rise,' she lied quickly.

His eyes glittered. 'I allow everyone one mistake, Kitty—but only one. Come, I'll show you inside.'

She followed him up the marble steps. She must pull herself together—stop crediting him with powers of perception he couldn't possibly have. He didn't have the power to read her mind; he was just an ordinary man.

No, she corrected herself silently, her eyes swinging automatically to watch the well-shaped line of his buttocks, revealed in all their muscular beauty in the white shorts. Not an ordinary man at all. He had something which would always mark him out in a crowd, and it wasn't just the outstandingly good looks, or the superb physique, or even that cool, calculating mind. He seemed to radiate some inner strength, some steely quality at the very heart of him. He looked, she thought, more than a little apprehensively, as though he did not have one vulnerable bone in his entire body...

He led her into a large entrance hall. 'Right,' he said briskly. 'That door over there is my study. I don't care to be disturbed when I'm in there working. Not for *any* reason. Understand?'

She nodded, her eyes still taking in the vastness of the hall.

'The main sitting-room is next door to the dining-room and over there——' he pointed '—is the kitchen. I'll get Simon to show you over properly later, once you've had a chance to settle in. I'd show you myself, but right now I'm a little tied up.'

At that moment, the door of another room opened and an incredibly pretty woman in her late twenties came out.

This was obviously what was tying him up, thought Kitty. His tennis partner. And what a stunner!

The woman was also wearing tennis whites—a short, pleated white skirt which showed off her long, evenly tanned legs. And, even though they had obviously just finished playing, she was clearly one of those women who didn't sweat. She looked as cool as a cucumber, with not a hair of the shiny brown ponytail out of place, not the merest hint of a shiny nose, nor the tell-tale sign of smudged mascara. Even her lipstick had remained unspoiled. Kitty loved sport herself, but her pale complexion inevitably flushed pink within the first ten minutes of playing.

Darius's partner turned her big brown eyes towards him, her hundred-megawatt smile for him alone.

He smiled back, his eyes crinkling at the corners. 'I won't be long,' he said. 'My new chef has just arrived. Kitty, this is Julia Davies. Julia—Kitty Goodman.'

'Hi,' grinned Julia. 'Pleased to meet you.'

She gave Kitty the once-over, but the friendliness in her face didn't waver.

She doesn't see me as a threat, thought Kitty suddenly. 'Hello,' she said, forcing herself to smile

back and quell the sudden rush of regret that she
hadn't been born tall and lovely. That her gingery
hair and accompanying freckles meant that breezily
beautiful women like Julia considered her no threat,
considered her safe to work around a man like
Darius.

'Don't give him too many carbohydrates, will
you?' laughed Julia. 'We don't want him piling on
the pounds.' And she gave Darius a playful punch
against a rock-hard torso which contained not a hint
of spare flesh.

'I'm just showing Kitty to her room,' said Darius.
'I'll only be a few minutes.'

'Fine. Mind if I take a shower?'

'Go ahead.'

And that, thought Kitty, spoke volumes about
the intimacy of their relationship.

'Bye, Kitty,' said Julia. 'I'll look forward to
sampling your cooking!' She gave another mega-
watt smile and walked off with a wiggle, disap-
pearing into a room at the end of the long passage.
To his bedroom? wondered Kitty.

There was a short pause as they watched her—
Kitty was dying to ask who the confident woman
who had eyed her so dismissively was, but Darius
was already speaking to her.

'Come with me and I'll show you where you'll
be staying.'

To her surprise, he walked straight through the
house and out at the other side, into a beautifully
informal garden whose vast size made her blink.
He weaved his way down a winding path onto which

a profusion of different-coloured flowers spilled, their hues like the contents of an artist's palette. He stopped at last in front of a building painted in an ice-cream-pink colour. It was a single storey only, and looked so cosy that it reminded Kitty immediately of an olde-worlde English cottage—she half expected to see hollyhocks and delphiniums growing around the door!

'I've put you in this annexe,' he said. 'I thought you might prefer it. It's completely self-contained.'

'The servant's quarters?' she murmured without thinking, then immediately wished she hadn't, for he fixed her with a sharp look.

'I thought that you might prefer the privacy. I have house guests staying sometimes—and as you'll be serving them with food and drink for a lot of the time I thought you'd like your own particular escape-valve.'

Her heart sank. The whole point of taking this job had been to give her access to his house. How on earth was she supposed to get to know the combination of his safe if she was situated miles away from the wretched thing? 'But what happens if they want drinks or snacks, say, in the middle of the afternoon?' she suggested brightly. 'Surely it would be much easier to have me—on tap, so to speak?'

His eyes narrowed at her unfortunate phrase, and she flushed scarlet to the roots of her hair.

'If they want anything between meals I can fix it. Or they can. I don't want you to be at my beck and call all day—that isn't the way I operate. You're employed to provide breakfast, lunch and dinner.

And sometimes tea mid-afternoon. And if that sounds like slave-labour, then remember—the nature of my job means I may have to go off for two or three days at a time, and you'll be completely free when I do.'

What alternative did she have other than to smile politely? 'That sounds very reasonable,' she said. Too reasonable. She'd have preferred a touch of the tyrant—tyrants were easier to dislike than reasonable men.

'It's now almost one,' he continued in that deep, drawling voice. 'Don't bother with lunch today. If you'd like to get yourself unpacked, I'll send Simon over in about an hour—he'll show you over the main house. You remember Simon?' he prompted, with an indefinable gleam lighting his grey eyes.

Yes, she remembered the tall, brown-haired secretary with whom she'd shared a short and somewhat awkward meal after her bizarre 'interview'—when he had steadfastly and neatly fielded any questions which might have given her a little more insight into the character of Darius Speed. Had he told his boss that she had seemed unusually interested in him? she wondered briefly, before discounting the thought. He probably hadn't thought to mention it—for wouldn't any prospective employee show a healthy interest in the man she would be working for, especially a man with the formidable reputation of Darius?

'Thanks,' she said, giving him what she hoped was another polite smile.

He nodded his dark head. 'I'll leave you to settle in. You have your own kitchen, which is fully stocked with everything I thought you'd need. Anything else, order it up through Simon. There's a swimming-pool in the grounds—please feel free to use it.' He began to turn away.

'And—when would you like me to start work?' she ventured.

He frowned distractedly, as if she had intruded on his thoughts. Glancing at the watch on his wrist, he paused. 'Let me see— I'm working on a script all day and I'm out to the theatre tonight. I'd like some sandwiches and tea at five-thirty, and supper for four after the show—just something cold which you can leave out. Nothing too fancy. Use what's available for tonight—you can shop tomorrow. And now,' he added, 'I'd better shower— I'm expecting a transatlantic call very shortly.'

She had a sudden, brief image of him showering. With Julia? Would the pretty brunette soon be slowly and sensuously rubbing lather all over that magnificent body of his...?

Kitty came back to the present to realise that she was studying the bronzed shafts of his muscular legs rather too closely, and she couldn't miss the tiny flash of discernment which briefly flared in the silver eyes as he acknowledged her scrutiny. A small smile played at the corners of his lips.

'Well, I think that's all. I'll see you at dinner— Kitty.' And he walked off back down the path the way they'd come, his tennis clothes dazzlingly and

starkly white against the deep, rich colours of the
flowers.

Oh, lord, thought Kitty, her eyes following him
with reluctant fascination. How on earth can I work
for him and how can I steal from him if I'm going
to start conjuring up disturbingly erotic fantasies
about him on day *one*?

CHAPTER THREE

KITTY'S hands were trembling as she pushed open the door and walked into the annexe, but her surroundings quickly lulled her into a calmer state, for it was impossible not to appreciate the comfort of the accommodation Darius had provided.

The sitting-room was deceptively large—but then she decided that perhaps the simplicity of the furnishings added to the illusion of space. The floors were of some pale wood which shone with the gleam of regular polishing. Several rugs were scattered here and there, woven with images which resembled some of the aboriginal paintings she had spotted in various Perth shops.

On the white walls were several large paintings depicting the Australian outback, whose vibrant colours dominated the room. They were all so exquisitely executed that she stood for a moment before one, completely lost in it. She saw the vivid cobalt-blue of a cloudless sky, contrasting with the deep dry red of the terrain, out of whose dust spiky, unfamiliar plants grew. She could imagine the harshness of that bleak and beautiful landscape. A different Australia, she thought as she gazed at it with rapt attention—and a world away from the sophisticated city she had seen so far.

Shaking herself out of her reverie, she explored the rest of the cottage. There was a bathroom with both bath and shower, a state-of-the-art kitchen, and a bedroom with a double bed in it... For one wild, unstoppable moment she imagined Darius Speed lying darkly naked against the stark white sheets. She wondered fleetingly if he made love as beautifully as he made films...

Oh, for goodness' sake! She was becoming obsessed with thinking about sex—she, with the sexual experience of a gnat!

What was important was that she was *here*, ready to put her plan into action and to do a big favour for Caro.

Kitty owed a lot to Caro. The rather eccentric sixty-five-year-old had rescued her from the deadly-dull highway snack-bar where Kitty had been working ever since she'd arrived in Western Australia on a working holiday, feeling utterly miserable and determined to forget all about Hugo. Caro had employed her as a temp in her own employment agency, Caro's Kitchen Cookies. Caro was friendly and clucky and Kitty adored her—and if the jobs she'd been sent on weren't up to much, well, at least they'd been thankfully brief and a whole lot better than the highway snack-bar. Kitty had shied away from permanent work, thinking that it might be too restrictive, but soon she'd begun to hanker after something which would allow her to use her culinary skills, instead of zooming round carrying a tray all day.

Then one day Caro had announced that she had the perfect permanent job—'but I can't possibly send you on it.'

'Why not?' Kitty had wanted to know.

'Because it's working for Darius Speed—the cheating swine!'

That's when the whole story had come out about Darius Speed stealing Caro's film-script.

'I sent it to him in good faith!' she'd quavered. 'It was *brilliant*—and now I hear he's making it into a film, with not a cent to me, or even a mention!'

Kitty had begged to go on the interview. 'I'm going to get your script back for you, Caro,' she'd said coolly.

'Could you *really*?' Caro's hands had fluttered as she'd waved her cheroot in the air. 'But you will be careful, won't you?' she'd twittered. 'He can be very devious, you know.'

'Well, I can be devious too,' muttered Kitty aloud as she began to undo the zip of her suitcase. 'Taking advantage of an old lady, indeed!'

She quickly hung her clothes up and filled the drawers with underwear, swimsuits and T-shirts, and checked her reflection in the mirror. She was wearing cobalt-blue leggings and a short-sleeved silk shirt of exactly the same colour. A casual outfit, and one which was entirely suitable for cooking, particularly when protected by one of the deep blue cotton smocks she usually wore for working.

She unpacked her various lotions and potions in the bathroom, before glancing at her watch. It would, in normal circumstances, she thought rather wistfully, be absolutely wonderful to have a swim in the pool he'd mentioned. But these were not normal circumstances, and it was important that she didn't lose sight of that for a moment. Important that she stayed on her guard where Darius Speed was concerned...

She glanced at her watch again. It had only taken her twenty short minutes to unpack, and Darius had said that Simon would be around in an hour.

Her sneaker-clad foot tapped lightly on the wooden floor and, as the minutes ticked by, she became sorely tempted to go and explore the house for herself.

Why bother waiting for Simon to come and show her around? Why not show a little initiative? She would go and explore the kitchen in the main house, decide what to cook for the evening meal, and maybe—just maybe—catch a glimpse of where he kept his safe...

She walked back along the perfumed path and into the main house, revelling in its cool, dim interior. The floors here were marble—she'd never seen marble floors in a private house before—and there was something so ancient and classical about them that she found herself having to resist an urge to slip her canvas shoes off, to feel the polished stone cool and smooth beneath her bare feet.

The house was also quiet.

Very quiet.

She stood still for a moment, listening, her head cocked to the side like a bird which suspected that a cat lurked near by. There was not a single sound to be heard.

Kitty made up her mind instantly, reminding herself of all the maxims learnt in childhood— about no time like the present, he who hesitates is

lost...so why waste an opportunity which might
not arise again for some days? Darius was in the
shower, which meant that the study was free. And
the study was probably where he kept his safe...

A number of doors led off the large main hallway
and she moved lightly towards the door she thought
he had said was his study, pausing as she gave the
gentlest of taps, which went unanswered, so,
pushing it quietly open, she stepped inside, her heart
sinking with disappointment as she noted that it
was a light, airy sitting-room whose doors opened
on to the veranda. Not a sight of a safe to be seen...

She retraced her steps back into the hall, her eyes
scanning the doors anxiously, as if she hoped that
their closed exteriors might provide her with some
clue. Like a small painted notice saying 'safe'—
perhaps with a convenient arrow? she thought with
a trace of humour as she knocked at a second door,
her heart lifting as she walked inside and saw walls
lined from ceiling to floor with books. Eureka! She
saw a huge high-backed chair with its back to her
which presided over a vast antique desk. His study,
she thought with relief.

And then, to her absolute horror, the chair slowly
swung round and, facing her, the quicksilver eyes
as cold as mercury itself, the mouth unsmiling, sat
Darius, his dark hair in damp tendrils, a telephone
receiver cradled between neck and shoulder and—
oh, horror of horrors—he was wearing nothing but
a short, dark towelling robe which gave her a
provocative glimpse of taut, hair-roughened thigh
and an equally disturbing view of a dark, muscular torso.

'Hello, Kitty.' The deep voice was very quiet, a strange undertone to it which filled her with instinctive foreboding. 'Looking for something?'

She thought, desperately, that her guilt must be written all over her frozen stance. If her intentions had been innocent, she would have been able to shrug and laugh it off, but, as it was, she didn't like the way he was looking at her one bit.

She decided quickly to brazen it out. 'Sorry,' she said guilelessly. 'I was looking for the kitchen.'

'I pointed it out to you earlier. Remember?' he prompted sarcastically.

'I'd—forgotten,' she improvised quickly.

'But that's precisely why I instructed Simon to give you a guided tour,' he snapped back. 'I thought I told you to wait for him to collect you?'

'Er—so you did,' she said lamely as she tried to think of a reasonable-sounding excuse, but quite honestly the sight of his body, obviously stark-naked beneath the robe, had put paid to any powers of reasoning remaining intact.

'So why didn't you?' he barked out at her, as though she were some kind of imbecile.

'Because I——' But she didn't have a chance to formulate an answer.

'Listen,' he cut across her, his voice as cold as his silver-grey eyes. 'Did you ever stop to wonder why I took so long before I interviewed you?'

'It had crossed my mind,' she admitted. 'I thought you'd probably found someone else you preferred.'

'What an attractive idea, Kitty,' he said softly. 'But unfortunately, unless I employed some well-established prima donna, there was no one nearly as good as you. And the reason I took so long was that I'm very fussy about who I allow in my home—and therefore I needed to write to England for your references.'

'But I sent you my references!' she protested.

'Which weren't worth the paper they were written on,' he ground out uncompromisingly. 'It's a common enough trick among people working abroad to forge their testimonials.'

Kitty's mouth fell open. In the circumstances, what right did *he* have to accuse *her* of being a cheat?

'I was satisfied with the information I received from England,' he continued relentlessly. 'As I was satisfied that you were reliable enough to carry out simple instructions. When I told you to wait, you damned well should have waited!'

Kitty set her mouth into a truculent line. 'I was using my initiative!' She glowered at him.

The silver eyes never left hers. 'Well, don't.'

And at this cursory order her vague stirrings of anger bubbled right over, even as she recalled his earlier instructions that he wasn't to be disturbed in his study. 'Oh, I'm so sorry,' she snapped, tossing her red plaits back over her shoulders. 'Is this room out of bounds or something?'

He said nothing for a moment, just allowed quicksilver eyes to travel over her face, resting for long seconds on her mouth with such intensity that she was afraid that she had some speck of dust on it or something, and her tongue snaked out to circle wetly round her lips.

'Not necessarily,' he said softly, his eyes still on her lips.

Oh, lord. He was *so* gorgeous. She suddenly forgot his high-handed and autocratic manner—forgot everything. Because, with his eyes homing in on her mouth like that, she felt as though he was actually kissing her, such was the potency of his magnetic stare. Tiny goose-pimples broke out beneath the thin blouse; she could feel her nipples begin to harden and scrape against the lace of her brassiere, and colour surged into her cheeks—because what if he noticed *that*? 'Could you direct me to the kitchen—please?' she asked breathlessly, desperate to get away from him and from this temporary insanity which had invaded her.

'You'll have to wait.' He nodded to a chair directly opposite him, on the other side of the desk. 'Sit down. I'm waiting for a call.'

She was reluctant to do as he asked, still afraid that those perceptive eyes would see the way her body was reacting to him, although the almost painful hardening of her breasts had already begun to subside. 'Then if it's confidential——'

'I'd say so,' he interrupted impatiently. 'Sit down.'

She had no alternative other than to obey him, looking down into her lap as she laced her fingers together—wondering how she could have been so naïvely stupid as to think she could just waltz in on her first day, grab the script, then disappear. And now she had probably alerted him, had probably made him suspicious. She looked up to find his eyes on her, and she gave him a polite half-smile, which went unanswered.

She was forced to sit there in silence and wait while he conducted what was evidently a high-powered conversation with some major studio backer in Los Angeles, and she gathered, from his cool, clipped replies, that he was refusing to back down on a particular point concerning finance. Her impression of film directors as unworldly, artistic and dreamy individuals flew right out of the window—this guy could evidently juggle figures with ease, and eat bankers for breakfast!

Eventually he replaced the receiver, and directed his attention at her again. He stood up. 'Shall we go?' he asked in a decidedly abrupt tone.

Kitty gulped and nodded, going through the door as he stood aside to let her pass, almost jolting from the sensation which rocked her as their arms brushed against one another, and then wondering if he must think her completely crazy, for his eyes narrowed as he stared down at her, observing the rigid movement of her arm as she pulled it away from him; but he said nothing.

He led the way down a larger corridor off the hall, before throwing open the door of the kitchen.

'Remember now?' he enquired, and she couldn't miss the searching stare he gave her.

Banishing wishes that she had never agreed to come to this house, to take part in such a potentially foolish escapade, she fixed him with a brilliant smile. 'Thanks. I won't forget again.'

'I'm sure you won't,' he drawled, then, to her utter amazement, he took her chin between his thumb and forefinger and stared down at her, and at that moment reality fled from her life as though it had never before existed.

It was like all the old fairy-stories, only more so—because she had never believed in them before.

His touch was just—magic.

Cool yet warm.

Firm yet gentle.

He tipped her head back a little and she was transfixed by the blinding blaze of the silver-grey eyes, unable now to stop the trembling of her mouth as it parted, as if impelled by him to do so...waiting...waiting...waiting...

His eyes gleamed and he nodded, as if satisfied. 'Yes,' he said slowly. 'It's very powerful. You feel it too. Don't you?'

'Feel—wh-what...?' she stammered.

He gave a click of impatience, the gleam leaving his eyes, and as the light left them they became as cold and as impersonal as if they'd been fashioned from metal.

'Oh, come *on*, Kitty,' he murmured. 'Don't deny what your body accepted minutes ago. Because you can't, can you? Your eyes are begging me to kiss you, aren't they?'

'N-no. They aren't,' she lied ineffectually.

He smiled. 'And do you know, I'm very tempted? *Very* tempted indeed!'

He was teasing, playing games with her—he must be. And it hurt. Gorgeous, world-famous film directors didn't feel tempted to kiss girls like her. 'Try it,' she said shakily, over-reacting by a mile, 'and I'll slap your face.'

He laughed. 'That might be interesting—purely for its novelty value,' he murmured arrogantly.

She brought her chin up as her eyes flashed angrily at him.

'Go on, then.' His voice had dropped to a deep, dark caress, and Kitty felt her breasts tighten with the tingle of anticipation. 'I dare you. Slap my face.'

She stared back at him, unable to move, her mind at odds with her body as she forgot all about Caro and why she was here, forgot all about everything other than the need to know what kissing him really *would* be like.

And, oh, heavens, she was just about to find out as that devastating dark head dipped down towards hers and his mouth found her lips.

For a second, there was a blaze inside her heart as she realised that the man whose face had graced a thousand movie-goers' magazine covers was actually kissing *her*—Kitty Goodman with the ginger hair. It was every woman's fantasy come to brazen, beautiful life.

And then she forgot just *who* she was kissing; her attention and her senses were all caught up with just *how* he was kissing. It was a soft, slow exploration, with scarcely any pressure on her mouth to begin with and with nothing but their lips touching at all. Which all changed when he shifted his head just a fraction to give him greater access to the moist, eager interior of her mouth, and she slipped her hands up to clutch at his shoulders as his tongue flicked with sensual ease to lick at hers, as though he were slowly licking cream off the top of a pudding.

She felt that pleasurable ache as the tips of her breasts clamoured into disbelieving life, her eyelids falling helplessly over her eyes, so, so tempted to move her hands down from his shoulders, to slip them inside his towelling robe and to touch and caress his bare chest...

And then he stopped kissing her, and stood staring down at her thoughtfully as she fought to drag some air into her starved lungs. To her horror she discovered that her desires had become actions and that her palms were lying against the hard nakedness of his chest, fingers fanned out over his nipples in as provocatively inviting and sexually possessive a gesture as it was possible to make.

'Oh, God!' she cried, wrenching her hands away with lightning speed.

A slow smile curved his mouth. 'I'm still waiting,' he murmured softly.

'W-waiting for what?' Not to make love to her *here*, surely?

'Why, for you to slap my face,' he concluded arrogantly.

She was stung, shocked, ashamed; a red mist of fury swam before her eyes, and she swung her hand up to hit him, but he was too quick for her, easily capturing her small wrist in his hand.

'Not *now*, Kitty,' he admonished sardonically. 'That's what's known as shutting the stable door after the horse has bolted, wouldn't you say?' And he waved his hand in the direction of a state-of-the-art cooker, and gave her an amused smile. 'I'll leave you to your cooking. I don't know about you, but I seem to have worked up the most *enormous* appetite.'

CHAPTER FOUR

KITTY'S fingers inflicted cruel punishment as she slammed the dough down yet again on the flour-covered marble board which lay on Darius's pristine work-surface.

What an utterly stupid, *stupid* thing to do, she told herself, her hands moving in time with her thoughts as she viciously kneaded the bread she was making. Darius had wanted sandwiches—well, she would give him sandwiches to die for!

She closed her eyes briefly. What *had* she been thinking of, sneaking around the house like a second-rate sleuth in an amateur-dramatic society's annual production?

And not just that, she reminded herself as the heel of her hand came down hard on the elastic mixture. Because then... Her cheeks flared with remembered chagrin. Then she had displayed the kind of fawning behaviour which was on a par with the woman in the black dress in the restaurant—the one with the ridiculous name—whose behaviour at the time *she* had so despised. Going ga-ga just because he'd touched her—even though he was thoroughly disreputable. No, far worse than that, she hadn't just gone ga-ga, she'd gone *completely* overboard. And if he hadn't stopped kissing her, she probably would have been tugging at the belt of that too-short robe to get her hands on even

44

more of that smooth brown flesh. What must he
have thought? Or was his spell over women so mes-
meric that any woman taken into the arms of Darius
Speed was doomed to behave so pathetically?

Kitty pounded the dough. What had happened
back there? She'd seen stars, heard violins, swooned
in his arms—all the things which were supposed to
happen when you fell...

She shook her head and actually laughed aloud.
Now she really *was* letting her imagination run away
with her. All that had happened was that the king
of seducers had given her a taste of his con-
siderable expertise at kissing. Imagine all the women
he must have kissed over the years. Small wonder
that a brief demonstration should act as such a
powerful aphrodisiac. Although it was a little
shaming to have been such a *walk-over*—why, she'd
gone out with Hugo for nearly six months and her
reactions towards him couldn't have been more
different...

She took a deep breath as she covered the dough
with a damp tea-towel and put it to one side to rise,
looking up as she heard the kitchen door open, her
hackles rising protectively as she steeled herself for
Darius.

But it was Simon who smilingly appeared, his
shiny brown hair gleaming, dressed in the habitual
Australian male summer uniform of knee-length
shorts worn instead of trousers, teamed with accompanying long socks. He had a pleasant face with
regular features and none of the brooding watchfulness of his employer. In the normal course of
events Simon was, Kitty decided, the kind of man

who would never have a problem with women—but she suspected that he would always play second fiddle to the colder, harder but infinitely more attractive Darius.

'Hi!' His eyes lit up. 'How's it going?'

'Great, thanks,' said Kitty, relaxing instantly, thinking what a pleasant and genuine smile he had.

There was something almost of the big brother about Simon—not that she had any brothers to compare him with, of course, but he made her feel somehow safe—the very opposite to how her boss made her feel.

Was she at ease with Simon simply because they'd shared a meal that evening? Because they were both in the subordinate roles of employees? Or was it because he seemed so uncomplicated and easy-going when compared with Darius?

Or maybe, she thought ruefully, it was just that she needed an ally in a house where she was planning to break the law...

'What's cooking?' asked Simon as he reached for a wooden spoon which stood in a bowl full of chocolate sauce.

'Get *off*!' laughed Kitty as he slapped his hand away—aware that she could never have behaved so spontaneously with Darius.

'Looks delicious,' said Simon, peering into the bowl disappointedly as she continued to hold the spoon out of reach.

'Thanks. But you know what they say—one taste leads to another.' She waggled a finger at him. 'And then there won't be any left for dinner, now, will there?'

'Yes, Mummy!' Simon pulled a face. 'Then I guess I'll just have to wait until later.'

Her eyebrows shot up. 'You're having dinner with Darius tonight, are you?'

'Don't look so surprised—he's not above eating with the hired help, you know,' he laughed.

Kitty blinked to hide her confusion. She had imagined that Darius would be going to the theatre and then dining with a cluster of beautiful women. 'It's just that I thought...' Her voice tailed off, denying the truth even to herself—that she had actually been suffering pangs of jealousy about whom he was eating with. How Simon would laugh if he knew!

'Do you live here, then?' she asked.

Simon shook his head. 'Heavens no,— I don't want to live my life *completely* in the great man's shadow! I have a condominium just a couple of minutes away.'

Kitty didn't know whether to feel relieved or anxious about this. True, she wouldn't have the added scrutiny of Simon—but it *did* mean she'd be alone in the house with Darius for much of the time.

Or did it?

'Does anyone else live here?' she asked casually.

Simon looked amused. 'Like who?'

'Like Julia.'

'You've met Julia?'

Kitty nodded, careful to keep her face impassive. 'When I arrived—she and Darius had just been playing tennis.'

'Mmm. Julia's a sweetie—but no, she doesn't live here. Darius is the original free spirit.'

I'll bet he is, she thought viciously. 'Do you and Darius often dine together?' she asked.

Simon took a can of beer from the fridge, snapped the lid off, and drank half. 'Not that often. We're both going to the play, with Julia, because Darius is thinking of casting the leading actress in his new film—he might bring her back here afterwards for supper. But sometimes we have a strictly working dinner—he'll bounce a whole load of ideas off me—and it will masquerade perfectly as an enjoyable evening, not in the least bit like work. Because Darius is—as I'm sure you've noticed——' and his eyes twinkled knowingly '—not without charm.'

Oh, I'd noticed all right, she thought acidly. 'How do you two know each other?' she quizzed, aware that she was sounding nosy.

Today Simon was much more forthcoming than he had been that night in the restaurant. 'Oh, we go back years. We were at college together.' He gave a mock-sigh and grimace. 'But I was always a beta student, while Darius was definitely alpha. Quite sickening, really. He got straight As *and* he was director of the student review. In fact, he was offered a job directing by a touring English theatrical company while still at college, but he turned it down.'

'Good grief,' said Kitty faintly, reeling slightly from this impressive list of achievements. 'Why?'

Simon shrugged. 'He made more out of driving a truck part-time. And he needed the money badly.'

Kitty's lips closed into a firm, determined and disapproving line. 'Oh?' she enquired archly. 'For gambling and partying, no doubt.'

Simon shot her a funny look. 'You're kidding! He was chasing a dream, even then. He wanted to start up his own production company. He wanted to have total artistic control, to produce, direct, and eventually—to write.'

Or to filch other people's writing! Kitty angrily gave the sauce an unnecessary stir, feeling just a little confused. Simon seemed a decent enough sort of man, and yet he'd known, and remained loyal to, Darius through college. But then she expected that Darius kept his underhand dealings well-hidden from his secretary.

'Darius wants me to show you round the house,' he smiled. 'Seems you blundered into his study earlier. A word of warning, my lovely freckle-face— steer clear of the lion's den.'

Her heart had started pattering. 'Oh?' she said casually, hot on the scent of a clue. 'Why's that? Does he have some terrible secret lurking in there?'

'You could say that. His scripts. His ideas. And they're sacrosanct—even from me! That's why he keeps them locked away in a safe.'

Kitty's heart hammered. 'You make it sound like Fort Knox!' she joked weakly. 'And only he knows the combination, I suppose?'

Simon frowned. 'Don't be silly—I'm his assistant—of course I have to know it too. Now, are you ready to let me show you around?'

Kitty decided that she had quizzed Simon enough for one day. She didn't want *him* suspecting anything. 'Sure.'

But at that moment there was a sharp, peremptory ring which echoed through the house. Simon gave a sigh. 'Better go—the master summons.'

'Who, Darius?'

'Mmm—probably needs me to send a fax for him. He feigns ignorance of any piece of office equipment and yet he can take a car to pieces and reassemble it in seconds!'

'Thanks for the recommendation,' came a dry voice from the door, and both Kitty and Simon whirled round to find Darius standing and filling the doorway.

He had dressed, thank heavens, was Kitty's first thought, before realising that *whatever* he wore couldn't disguise that magnificent body. The short, dark towelling robe, which had revealed rather too much of that iron-hard physique, had been replaced by faded old jeans which looked as though they had been sprayed on... And his torso didn't fare much better. True, there was nothing actually *indecent* about the cap-sleeved white T-shirt but, oh, Lord, the *reality*. Every rippling muscle, every lean sinew was as clearly defined as if Michelangelo had taken a chisel and hammered it out of pure Carrara marble. She remembered how she'd covered his chest with her palms as he'd kissed her...

Kitty found herself colouring as she came back to the present to find the cold, metallic eyes on her, and she snapped out of reliving that kiss, but not a flicker of expression on the implacable features indicated that he'd noticed her discomfiture.

'Send a fax for me, would you, Si?'

'See?' Simon grinned at Kitty, then turned to Darius. 'But I thought you wanted me to show Kitty around the house.'

'I can do that,' came the dark voice, and there was an indefinable glint which momentarily hardened the silver eyes. 'Can't I, Kitty?'

He was like a chocolate-bar, thought Kitty—best kept well out of reach in case you succumbed to temptation... 'I don't mind waiting for Simon to finish,' she said steadily.

'I'm sure you don't,' came the quietly emphatic reply. 'But Simon has work to do. Don't you, Simon?'

'Sure,' said his secretary reluctantly, and disappeared from the kitchen.

'So, Kitty,' came that deep, soft voice, and Kitty mentally prepared herself for some mocking comment about that kiss. But to her astonishment there was none. All he said was, 'Ready to see over the house?'

'Certainly,' she replied, amazed that she could sound so calm when her heart was hammering away like crazy.

She followed him from the kitchen and into what seemed like an endless series of rooms. It was, she realised, deceptively large. Like many Australian houses, with land-space not such a problem as it was in England, it was built on a vast plot, with a shady veranda running around the entire bottom half of the building. Next door to the kitchen was the dining-room, where candles and silver were displayed on the table and fresh flowers scented the room.

'Who does all the cleaning?' asked Kitty suddenly, thinking that she was going to have her work cut out if it was down to her to keep this mammoth house looking neat and tidy.

There was a glimmer of a smile. 'Don't worry—not you. I have a delightful lady named Janet who comes in every day bar Sunday.'

'And what happens on Sunday?'

'I'm perfectly capable of loading and unloading a dishwasher,' he drawled.

A new man? she wondered sarcastically. 'But not of sending faxes?' she murmured.

'That's different—that's what I pay Simon for. Besides, he always remembers to file them away. Mine always get forgotten, or lost.'

He ran his hand through the thick, dark hair as he spoke and Kitty again felt terribly confused. What a mixture of contradictions this man was—genius director, financial wizard, lover *extraordinaire*, thief—and yet, just then, he'd looked and sounded like the archetypal absent-minded professor, losing papers all over the place, just waiting for an eager partner to cluck after him!

'Now here,' he continued as he flung open another door, 'is the drawing-room.'

Ah, yes. This was the room she had stumbled into earlier on her fruitless mission to find the safe.

He showed her the guest suite, situated on the ground floor, where Julia had disappeared to have her shower. So she hadn't used *his* bathroom! But there again, that didn't mean much. He was probably one of those fastidious men who wouldn't dream of letting anyone use his bathroom in case they pinched his dental floss! But then her eyes were drawn to how those narrow hips were exquisitely moulded by the faded, ridiculously scruffy denim, and she sighed as she rejected that last hypothesis. No, she could somehow see him as the kind of man who *shared* his dental floss!

He had elegantly placed one long leg on the bottom step of the staircase. 'Now come upstairs,' he said silkily, 'and I'll show you where I sleep.'

She stood stock-still against the wall beside the banister. 'No, thank you!' she said, before she could stop herself. 'That really won't be necessary.'

His eyes flicked over her. 'What a suspicious mind you have, Kitty. What did you think I was about to do—throw you down on the bed and have my wicked way with you?'

Her heart raced, but she kept her face calm. 'After your behaviour earlier, nothing would surprise me!'

He gave a low laugh which was strangely lacking in humour. 'What a little hypocrite you are. We both know what happened earlier. And we both know who brought matters to a halt. And if I hadn't——' he gave a lazy shrug '—who knows what would have happened?'

'Why, you—you...!' She searched around for the ultimate insult. 'You're no gentleman!' she spat out, thoroughly incensed by the truth behind his words.

'I never claimed to be,' he drawled. 'A "gentleman" always seems to me to be someone so conditioned by society's expectations that he doesn't have an original thought or feeling in his body.'

'But he has values—honourable values,' said Kitty stiffly. It was as close as she could get to an accusation without actually giving anything away, but he must have sensed the strange nuance in her tone, for his eyes suddenly narrowed and he stilled.

'I have a feeling,' he said thoughtfully, 'that we're having a two-way conversation here.'

Kitty quickly closed her eyes, then opened them again, afraid she'd said too much. 'I think I've seen as much of the house as I need to,' she said deliberately. 'Will you be needing me for anything else?'

The slight elevation of his eyebrows, the arrogant half-question in those silver eyes sent her blood pressure soaring.

'Nothing you'd approve of, I'm sure,' he said cryptically and, turning on his heel, swung his gorgeous denim-clad hips in the direction of his study.

Kitty hurried back to the kitchen where she put the bread in to bake and made a salmon and spinach roulade for supper, to be followed by a chocolate mousse.

After she'd finished she drank a can of ice-cold cola, thoroughly shaken, her nerves shattered. The sooner she had achieved her objective and was out of there the better. What *was* it about the man that he could make such provocative statements and then have her actually wondering what it would be like to be thrown down on the bed and made love to?

She put her glass in the dishwasher and made her way back to her annexe. She was strung up, and Darius's suggestion to use the pool seemed like a good idea. Perhaps some physical exercise would quell the strange unfamiliar aching inside her which wouldn't seem to go away...

Changing into the pale blue swimsuit she'd bought recently, Kitty draped a white towelling robe over her shoulders, slipped her feet into white deck shoes and made her way slowly towards the pool. There were trees here, shading the path, tall and graceful, their blossoms bright and exotic, and as the sunlight dappled through the flower-strewn branches, sending rippling shadows before her, she felt the sudden heightening of her senses, and, with it, a deep sense of regret.

She *should* be having the time of her life. Here she was, staying in a country of breathtaking beauty, and yet she was starting a crazy life of sub-terfuge. She had come to Australia to escape, not just from a broken love-affair, but from the close confines of her life in England. She had wanted new life and adventure breathed into her. She should be glorying in every moment of her working holiday here, whereas in reality that was not the case at all.

I must find the script as soon as possible, she decided as she padded towards the pool. Then get out. Leave Western Australia and explore the eastern side of this great continent. Get out, before I too fall under the spell of Darius Speed...

She reached the pool, guided by the dappled tur-quoise light which was reflected off the water, and spent an enjoyable half-hour of steady swimming, interspersed with the occasional foray to the depths of the cool, deep water, and, as she did so, all the latent tension which had lain coiled in the pit of her stomach gradually receded.

Eventually, she started to haul herself up the steps, blinking a little in the fierce sunlight, when something stopped her.

Beneath the shadows of a flame-tree which dominated one side of the pool, a still and watchful figure was draped on a lounger, a film-script lying on his lap, head leaning back against his hands as he studied her through half-closed lids. But the relaxed pose was deceptive, Kitty could sense that, and she suddenly felt more out of her depth than she had done in the swimming-pool. In silence he watched as her water-slicked limbs slowly navigated the steps, and his wordless scrutiny made the tension within her return in an instant.

'You're trembling,' he observed.

'Yes.' Her teeth chattered like hail on a tin roof. She became suddenly aware that she stood before him almost naked. The pale blue swimsuit, which she had bought from one of the shops near Cottesloe, urged on by a young and trendy salesgirl, now seemed more indecent than fashionable. It was cut extremely high on the leg, which was the current vogue, the effect being to create an illusion of long legs—and Kitty needed all the help she could get! But somehow, with the suit all wet and clingy after her swim, she became aware that it carefully moulded the swell of her breasts, from fleshy mound to erect nipple; it even outlined the slight curve of her belly, dipping down into her navel, exposing her so that she might as well have been wearing nothing at all.

'Here.' He put the film-script down and stood up, picking up her robe from the nearby lounger and tossing it to her. 'Put this on.' His voice sounded almost harsh as it barked out the order, and her fingers were trembling as she did as he told her. She was unable to look away from that searching gaze which made her wish that she could pull a veil over her thoughts. She suddenly understood what people meant when they said, 'It was as though the rest of the world didn't exist.' Because for Kitty, standing there, damp and shaking, nothing existed bar the tall man in the faded jeans who stood before her, his thighs apart, his hands splayed over narrow hips in an unconscious but blatantly sensual stance.

A strange silence descended on them, enveloped them, and Kitty felt unconsciously drawn towards him; she had to force herself to remember that she wasn't supposed to feel like this about him. He had committed the unspeakable crime of stealing from a dear old lady. She cleared her throat. 'You aren't swimming, then?' she ventured, seeking refuge in the kind of conventional comment she would normally make, anything which would stop him looking at her like *that*.

'No, I'm not swimming.' The huskiness had gone; the neutrality of his normal voice had returned.

'Don't you ever do anything but work?' she asked curiously, her eyes flicking over to the film-script, wondering whether that was his work—or someone else's.

'You mean all work and no play...?' he mocked.

She hadn't meant that at all. And she didn't like that soft tone of seductive mockery—or, rather, she did—too much. It made all kinds of dark, illicit and sexy thoughts lap through her mind's eye, like an incoming tide...

She fought again to keep the feelings at bay. 'Don't you like to swim?' It should have been chatty; it sounded inane.

His eyes gleamed silver; his hair gleamed jet. 'I swim every morning, and again before dinner. It helps keep me fit.'

She forced her eyes not to stray to his flat torso, imagining him ploughing with relentless strength through the water. Like a machine, she thought suddenly. This man would swim for exercise, rarely for pleasure. This was not a man who would linger by warm rock-pools to explore within, or spend long hours splashing around with a beach-ball just for the hell of it. He had, she realised suddenly, all the capacity for sensual enjoyment of the water, but neither the time nor the inclination for it. He was driven by some demon, something which quashed the sybarite within him—he was not a man whose flesh clamoured for over-indulgence.

I'm cracking up, she thought as she made to turn away, but a movement of his hand stilled her.

'Why?' he asked softly.

Guilt caused soft colour to stain her cheeks. For heaven's sake—had he *guessed*? 'Why—what?' she stumbled.

'Why do you look at me in that way?'

'What way's that?' She tried to inject bemused humour into her voice, but she failed miserably.

His mouth expelled a long, thoughtful breath of air. 'As though . . . as though you don't trust me. And yet you hardly know me. Almost . . .' his voice had softened to a whisper, his eyes perplexed '. . . as if you're afraid of me.'

Uneasiness at his perception fizzled through her, but then she thought of Caro, and her chin came up in defiance. 'And are women never afraid of you?' she challenged.

'Sometimes,' he admitted. 'Very occasionally. But never without good cause. Do you, Kitty——' and he looked down into her face '——have good cause to be afraid of me?'

She giggled with sheer nerves, and the giggle somehow restored conventionality, for he also smiled, and with the smile returned the mask of the heart-breakingly handsome man who was nigh-on irresistible.

'How could I have?' she answered, determinedly casual. 'I only met you for the first time the other evening.'

But the suspicion had not quite left his eyes. 'You don't have journalistic talents, I suppose?' he mused.

She stared back uncomprehendingly. 'Meaning?'

'If you've got yourself this job thinking that you'll do an in-depth profile for one of the women's glossies, then I'd advise you not to bother,' he warned. 'The contract you signed has a privacy clause. And——' the silver eyes glittered '—it's watertight.'

She attacked. It seemed the only thing to do. 'You seem to have such a poor opinion of my motives for taking this job, Darius, that frankly I'm surprised that you employed me in the first place.'

'Because you were the best,' he said softly. 'Without doubt. And I'm used to the best.'

I'll bet you are. She decided to call his bluff. 'Well, now that I've arrived, you seem to be having second thoughts. If you want to terminate my employment then go ahead. I promise you I shan't break down in tears.'

His face remained indifferent. 'But that would be too easy, Kitty,' he mocked. 'Something about you puzzles me, perplexes me. And I like puzzles.' He gave a wolfish smile. 'Solving them, that is.'

She gave a bemused little shake of the head. 'I'm afraid that you've lost me. Now——' a bright smile '—I'd better go and change,' she said hastily, before she got herself in any deeper.

'So you had,' he said impassively.

And Kitty fled, her heart beating nervously, away from the searching look that lay in the depths of those strange grey eyes.

CHAPTER FIVE

KITTY rushed back to her annexe and went straight to the bathroom to strip off her damp swimsuit.

She shivered just before stepping underneath the warm jets of the shower—and it had nothing to do with the cold. Was Darius as perceptive as his questions to her had seemed to indicate? He had seemed to suspect that she wasn't everything she claimed to be—or was she just being paranoid?

Drying herself on the huge, fluffy bath-sheet, Kitty wandered naked into her bedroom, pausing fractionally in front of the full-length mirror as she remembered the way that he'd subjected her to a slow scrutiny with those assessing silver eyes. And even as she remembered it she saw, to her horror, that her nipples had tightened into two pointed rosy peaks and she coloured furiously as she quickly stepped into black briefs and snapped on a matching bra.

Dear heaven, she thought helplessly, what in the world is happening to me?

She pulled the zip of her black denims up with a defiant jerk. She needed to act fast. Before he suspected even further—and what better time than tonight? Fate had fortuitously sided with her, and Darius was leaving her alone in his house. Time enough for her to suss out how the land lay.

She took him a tray of Earl Grey tea and old-fashioned egg and cress sandwiches at five-thirty, as requested. He was in the sitting-room, lying sprawled on the sofa, his position emphasising the lean thrust of his thighs, and Kitty had to blink several times as she made the reluctant observation of how utterly dynamic he looked in the dark, formal dinner-jacket. But once again, as he'd done at her interview, he had added a touch of originality to make him look eye-catchingly different. Instead of the usual plain black bow-tie, his was in a pale, gleaming silver which echoed his eyes and made him look like some kind of delectable maverick.

'Your sandwiches,' said Kitty stiffly.

'Thanks.'

'Shall I pour?'

'Mmm. Do. It's one of those things that women do so much better, don't you agree?' he mocked.

'Oh, yes,' she retorted sarcastically. 'It takes a certain kind of particularly *feminine* skill to up-end a teapot. Milk or lemon?'

He laughed. 'Neither, thanks.' He accepted the cup. 'Fiery little thing, aren't you? Must be the hair.'

'Am I?' she answered back coolly, though the sound of that dark, treacly voice was making her feel about as cool as a hothouse flower! 'Sandwich?'

'Thanks.'

She'd made the sandwiches the way they were supposed to be made—dainty, crustless triangles— but Darius immediately demolished two of them with an appreciative hunger which seemed suddenly very earthy. Kitty backed away.

'If there's nothing else, I'll be leaving your supper in the fridge. I hope you enjoy the play!' she said with false brightness as those all-knowing silver eyes narrowed thoughtfully.

Kitty escaped from the house and into the garden, glancing at the large chunky Mickey Mouse watch on her wrist as she did so. Darius had told her he was leaving at six-thirty and would be back at ten-thirty. That gave her four hours in which to find his safe—heaps of time.

Just quite how she was going to open it once she'd found it she didn't know—but she remembered seeing an old Peter Sellers film once. Didn't you just press your ear against the door and wait for a faint but tell-tale click as you hit the right number? That's what she'd try, anyway!

Except that it didn't quite turn out that way...

As soon as she heard the low, throaty growl of the black Porsche she'd seen parked in the driveway, Kitty bolted into the house and straight into the study, standing in the book-lined room momentarily to catch her breath, when there was a loud ring on the doorbell.

Blast it! Kitty hesitated. Maybe if she didn't answer it the person would just go away.

Another, longer ring told her that this was a false hope and, resignedly, Kitty stomped out into the impressive hall and pulled open the front door.

There stood a Junoesque blonde of almost six feet tall, who looked about nineteen. She had vermilion lips and blonde hair falling down over a

T-shirt which bore the legend 'I'm too sexy for my clothes' together with denim shorts cut right up to her bottom.

'Hi!' she said cheerfully. 'I'm Janet!'

'Janet?' echoed Kitty blankly.

'Yeah. I clean for Darius.'

'His *cleaner*?' The girl looked more like model material than someone who would wield a mop around the place, thought Kitty.

Janet obviously knew this, since she acknowledged Kitty's surprise with a broad grin. 'Well, it's only to support myself through uni,' she confided. 'I'm studying film-making—I'm kind of like Darius' protégée.'

'Really?' said Kitty archly, trying to repress the spear of indignation which shot through her as she attempted not to imagine just what sort of services the youthful beauty had to provide to earn his patronage. She found Janet staring at her rather curiously.

'Darius just dropped by on his way to the theatre. Said you might welcome some company as you didn't know anyone in Oz.'

Or was he very subtly having her watched? thought Kitty immediately, opening the door wider to let the blonde beauty breeze through.

Janet helped herself to a bottle of wine from the fridge and fetched two glasses out of a cabinet in the dining-room, and Kitty followed her like a lost sheep.

It would be churlish, she decided, if she didn't make *some* effort to chat to Janet, who actually turned out to be very engaging and friendly.

And very frank.

'Of course, I'm *madly* in love with Darius,' she sighed, pushing some thick, blonde hair back off her shoulder.

'Does he know?' asked Kitty.

'Oh, yes, I should think so. Occupational hazard for him. I've known him since I was sixteen.'

'*Sixteen*?'

Janet nodded. 'He came to our school to give a talk, saw some of my work and said I had talent. Trouble is, that was four years ago. I'm twenty now. I keep waiting for him to notice that I've grown up. But he hasn't.'

Kitty thought that, with her long legs spread out like a colt's and her wistful face, Janet didn't look at all grown-up. She put her glass down on the table and stifled a put-on yawn.

'Janet, it's been lovely talking to you, but I'd really like to turn in now. It's only my first day and I still have some unpacking to do.'

'OK,' said Janet easily. 'Shame, though—I've enjoyed meeting you.'

It was nearly nine o'clock by the time Kitty had ushered Janet out of the house. And there she'd been thinking that fate was on her side...

She spent a fruitless half-hour in the study, searching high and low for some evidence of a safe. It might have helped if she'd ever seen one in real life!

She sat back on her heels in the middle of the room and could have howled with frustration. Simon had told her that the safe was in Darius's study—but what if that was a security measure? What if Simon had been lying?

She racked her brains. Where else could he keep it if not in his study? Somewhere private...

Like his bedroom?

Dared she?

In an instant she'd made her mind up, thinking about Caro, still struggling at over sixty in her employment agency, while he lived like a king and swanned off to the theatre at the drop of a hat.

She ran up the staircase and set about finding his bedroom—easily done, since it was very large and very masculine, with a magnificent picture window which overlooked the grounds and through which the brilliant light of the moon made the room appear as bright as day.

It didn't look as she'd imagined a film director's bedroom would look. Apart from the size and the quality of the fittings, it was very—well, *ordinary* really. There were no mirrors, or black satin sheets. Or revolving beds... Kitty gulped. Of course there *was* a bed, and a very large and comfortable bed it looked, too.

She suddenly felt like Goldilocks, filled with a crazy and overwhelming urge to climb beneath the sheets and wait for him...

Wait for him?

With a jolt, she looked at her watch and saw with relief that it was just after nine-thirty. She still had nearly an hour.

Feeling like a criminal for the first time, Kitty pulled open the wardrobe door with a loud click, to be confronted by the sight of a pile of silk boxer shorts in a variety of colours.

Kitty swallowed, then froze as she heard the unmistakable sound of the front door slamming, then voices floating upwards, one of them very deep and unmistakably belonging to Darius.

Her chilled hand fell from the wardrobe door-handle and, to her horror, the door swung back into place with an ominously loud click which sounded to a fraught Kitty like a bomb going off.

She held her breath, letting it out in a long, steady sigh as she heard the voices moving, heard the chink of ice against crystal which meant that they were all having drinks.

She would wait here until they were all busy drinking and eating and chatting, and then she would slip quietly down unnoticed, back to her annexe.

Dear lord! Cold beads of sweat made the back of her neck clammy, and the palms of her hands felt suddenly icy. What was he doing back so early?

And then she nearly died as the moon moved behind a cloud and the room was suddenly cloaked in terrifying darkness, just as the bedroom door swung slowly open and a large, dark figure stood silhouetted against the landing light. In her fright, she took a stumbling step back and opened her mouth to scream, when she was pushed back on the bed and a lean, hard body landed on top of her, knocking all the breath out of her.

As though he'd stage-managed it, the cloud lifted and the silver light streamed in to illuminate Kitty lying helplessly under a very angry Darius.

'*You*!' he snarled, the angles of his face all harsh, distorted lines. 'What in God's name do you think you're doing in my bedroom?'

She was frightened of his anger; frightened too of the uncomfortable awareness of how her body was reacting to his pinning her down so firmly against his bed.

'Answer me!' he demanded.

'I thought—I thought I heard the sound of an intruder!' she babbled.

His lip curled. 'So did I. It seems I was right. I'm afraid you'll have to do better than that, Kitty.'

'No, honestly—I swear it!' She crossed her fingers behind her back. 'After Janet had left, I was about to put the glasses in the dishwasher when I heard a sound from upstairs, and I thought it might be a burglar.'

'So you took the most sensible course of action and came tripping up here, all one hundred and twenty undefended pounds of you, to confront our mystery invader?' he suggested sarcastically.

Kitty nodded eagerly.

'Whereas anyone with an ounce of common sense would have picked up a phone and dialled the police. You'll forgive me, Kitty, if I have a little trouble accepting your story.' He leaned over her to snap on the bedside lamp, rolling back to stare down at her, his eyes sweeping from her throat to her ankles, and Kitty prayed that he wouldn't notice the two insistently hard nipples which were straining through the thin material of her T-shirt. And just in case he did notice she crossed her arms protectively over her chest, like an indignant matron.

An assessing look came into his eyes as he noted the black jeans and T-shirt. 'Well, from the way you're dressed, you obviously weren't up here with seduction in mind.'

She took the opportunity to scramble off the bed. 'What's *that* supposed to mean?'

His mouth tightened into a derisory slash. 'It has been known for women to find out the where-abouts of my bed,' he said rawly. 'And to avail themselves of it, wearing a selection of what is termed, I believe, sexy underwear. Personally, I find it about as sexy as a cold shower—and it's just about the last thing which would entice me. Now tell me, Kitty.' And he sprang to his feet in a single, fluid movement, snapping his hand around her wrist and bringing her up close to him, before she could stop him. 'I'm asking you again. Just what were you doing sneaking around my bedroom?'

It was her word against his. She stuck her chin in the air defiantly. 'And I've already told you—I thought I heard a burglar!'

He gave a click of impatience. 'I don't believe you,' he said flatly. 'But I have neither the time nor the inclination to discuss it now. I have friends and an actress downstairs waiting for me.

'Be in my study before breakfast tomorrow morning,' he ordered. 'At eight o'clock. *Sharp*!'

CHAPTER SIX

KITTY lay awake for most of the night, finally
dropping off just as the pale light of dawn began
to steal in through a crack in the blue silk curtains.
When she sat up in bed, her eyes were gritty and
her head felt as though she'd had a hard night on
the town.

The chances were that she'd be unemployed as
of two minutes past eight and would be back at
Caro's Kitchen Cookies looking for new work.

She sighed as she pulled a mauve gingham mini-
dress down over her hips and slipped on matching
soft leather pumps. Oh, well—she'd given it her
best shot. Perhaps she could suggest that Caro persuade one of the local newspapers to take up her
case. Although if Darius got wind of it he could
easily destroy any evidence that Caro had written
the script, and probably sue them for libel.

She arrived at his study on the dot of eight, to
find him already deep in work, the sleeves of his
cambric shirt rolled up, his dark head bent over a
script—*Caro's* script? thought Kitty suddenly—as
he scored great lines through whole pages of text.

He looked up as she entered, and his grey eyes
were as cold as a winter sky. He didn't even ask her
to sit down.

He surveyed her in silence for a moment. 'I've
been thinking about last night's little *incident*,' he

said at last, and narrowed his eyes. 'I once told you that I allow people one mistake, and one only—well, that was yours, Kitty. One more and you're out.' The silver stare was as steady as the horizon, and he held a hand up to silence her as she opened her mouth to speak. 'I don't believe your story about hearing an intruder for a moment, and don't,' he warned, 'insult my intelligence by repeating it. I've already stressed that your contract has a privacy clause, so I'm confident that "The Secrets of Darius Speed's Boudoir" won't ever make it to the pages of a women's magazine.'

Just for one gloriously rebellious moment, Kitty imagined herself telling the world that Darius Speed owned a pair of lime-green boxer shorts!

'I'll put your presence there down to understandable feminine curiosity,' he said, with a condescending smile, 'and we'll leave it at that.'

Behind her closed lips, Kitty gritted her teeth and only prevented herself from grinding them together with an effort. Why, the patronising, arrogant *pig* of a man!

'That will be all, thank you, Kitty,' he said coolly, and, having been so summarily dismissed, she went off to the kitchen to fume as she prepared him some fresh fruit and coffee for breakfast.

He had basically left her with two choices. She could decide that she found his whole attitude intolerable, in which case she could leave right now.

But then an image sprang to mind, of Caro with her bright but hopelessly mismatched clothes, her eyes misting over as she told Kitty of how she had poured her heart and soul into her film-script.

'Honestly, Katherine,' she had sniffed, 'with all the money that man has, you wouldn't think that he could rob an old woman, would you?'

After twenty-four hours under the same roof, she could believe *anything* of the man, thought Kitty grimly as she fanned out some cool slivers of iced mango on the plate.

She had never believed that a man could have such a warped view of the human race! According to Darius, everyone he met was either out to land a job in one of his films or was trying to entice him into bed!

Unless, prompted the small voice of her conscience, it was true? What about Ffyona Arnold in the restaurant? And hadn't she seen Julia and Janet both swooning over him? Hadn't *she* done the same? *And* she seemed to have conveniently forgotten that she herself had eyed that large bed of his with distinctly avid curiosity.

No, she would stay. But he had given her only one more chance and, if she stayed, she had to quell his suspicions. She would have to excel—glitter and sparkle with wit and humour—well, if not exactly that, then at least she could try acting normally.

That way he might begin to trust her, and when she had gained his trust she would carefully observe his daily routine, and, at the first opportunity, *pounce*!

And acting normally would have to include losing this tendency to dissolve into a small heap at his feet every time he looked at her.

Spurred on by her renewed resolve, Kitty began to chop away at a heap of strawberries.

Winning Darius over, or at least banishing that thoughtful expression from his eyes whenever he looked at her, certainly wasn't easy. But what ground she did gain was done by the simple expedient of demonstrating her culinary skills.

She could tell that he was massively impressed with the dishes she produced every day—although he didn't exactly go overboard with praise. But he ate his food with a frank enjoyment, and his distant smile became a fraction less distant as the tantalising flavours of home-made dishes bombarded his taste-buds.

The way to a man's heart is through his stomach, thought Kitty one day at the end of her first week. Though the old saying certainly couldn't be applied to Darius. Since he had found her in his bedroom that night, any evidence of the powerful chemistry between them which he'd claimed had existed had vanished completely. At least, on his side it had.

But not on hers.

For Kitty, it was infuriating and frustrating that she had to suffer Darius in her dreams each night, usually half clothed and in a breathtakingly X-rated scenario. She would wake up with a pounding heart and dry mouth and pray that she'd get an opportunity to retrieve Caro's script very soon—before she did her health some serious damage.

Her days began to dissolve into their own kind of routine. Kitty was always free every afternoon and after supper. Most of her evenings she spent reading from the vast library of books, writing letters home or watching videos. Once she watched one of Darius's films with him and Simon, and afterwards he actually asked her opinion of it.

'Not your best,' she said bluntly.

He laughed. 'It was my first,' he said. 'You can tell.'

By day the house seemed to be littered with people. Simon was there most of the time, and Janet appeared in the kitchen during breaks from college when she was supposed to be cleaning the house. She *did* clean it—but she spent a hell of a lot of time drinking coffee and gossiping about the various men who were in and out of the house, comparing them all unfavourably with Darius.

Darius was holding talks with various freelance film-makers and looking at the work of other professionals who hoped to be hired by him. Kitty was always having to shoo people out of the kitchen. Every day she provided vast pots of curried chicken, chilli, lasagne—all of which were demolished as if by a plague of locusts. But she didn't join in with these particular lunches—she'd have ended up looking like a whale if she had!—so she'd nobly make herself a salad sandwich accompanied by a glass of mineral water which she often took down to the pool with a book, taking great care to sit in the shade.

It was here one day, while she was lying dozing, her hand dangling over the side of the lounger, that she felt the brush of soft fur against her hand, and she opened her eyes blinkingly to find a very young and exceptionally cute tortoiseshell cat staring coyly up at her.

She rubbed her finger behind the cat's ear, whereupon it obligingly turned over on to its back to await further ministrations.

'Now just who,' she wondered aloud, 'do *you* belong to?'

She didn't have to wait very long for her answer, for she heard a scuffling in the undergrowth and the muddy face of a small boy appeared. Kitty judged him to be about four years old.

He looked first at Kitty, then at the cat, then back again at Kitty in silent suspicion.

Kitty, whose knowledge of small boys could have been written on the back of a postage stamp, gave him a smile, but he continued to glare at her.

'Hello,' she said. 'What's *your* name?'

'Wayne,' he scowled.

He continued to stare at her with a belligerent expression.

'Well, Wayne—is this your cat?'

'Might be.'

'Either it is or it isn't,' she said reasonably.

''Tis. It didn't mean to get in your garden.'

'I'm sure it didn't. What's her name?'

'*His* name,' he corrected. 'Mersey. He's called Mersey. Me mam came from Liverpool,' he added, seeing Kitty's perplexed frown.

'And where do you and Mersey live?'

He jerked his head. 'Next door.'

Kitty resisted the urge to raise her eyebrows in surprise. If Wayne's family could afford to live in Jackland Parade, then she was surprised that his mother didn't dress him a bit better. It wasn't that he was muddy and scruffy—the little she *did* know about boys was that scruffiness was par for the course. But the boy's shorts were much too small for him, as was his T-shirt, and the toe-cap of one of his trainers had a hole in it.

'Does your mother know where you are?'

'Nah! She's out shopping. The old bag she works for is a slave-driver. I can look after myself.'

'Your mum works next door?'

'Yeah, for Mrs Rawlings.' His eyes narrowed. 'This your place?'

Kitty grinned. 'You must be joking! This is Mr Speed's house. I just work here.'

He grinned back, a bond established, before glancing down at the glittering turquoise water. 'Nice pool,' he said, with all the subtlety of a sledge-hammer.

'You must have one next door,' Kitty pointed out.

'Yeah, but old Ma Rawlings won't let me use it.'

'Why not?'

'She says I'd pee in the pool—that all boys——'

'Wayne,' interrupted Kitty in a stern voice, which was the only way she could keep from laughing. 'If I spoke to your mother and you promised *never* to pee in the pool, I can't see any reason why you shouldn't swim here from time to time—with me watching you, of course.'

'I can't swim,' he said glumly.

She smiled. 'I could always teach you.'

His face lit up like candles on a birthday-cake. 'But won't Mr Speed mind?' he came back quickly.

That was something she didn't want to think about—not now. Mr Cynical Speed would probably think that both Wayne *and* his mother were would-be actors.

Yes, all things considered, she could imagine Darius hitting the proverbial roof. She hesitated, not wanting to disappoint the little boy, and what the eye didn't see ... 'Mr Speed's a very busy man,' she prevaricated. 'So we won't bother him. It'll be our little secret.'

It did occur to her as she said it that her life was filling up with lots of little secrets of one kind or another...

Wayne came to the pool to be taught by Kitty a couple of times a week, and the irony was that by now she really *was* enjoying her job, and with each day that passed her conscience began to pluck away at her mind, like a learner's fingers on a violin-string.

Just when *was* Darius going to go away and leave her free access to the house? she wondered in some desperation. She tried asking Simon about it.

'He's got nothing definite in his schedule until he starts filming after Christmas, but there again he could jump on a plane to anywhere tomorrow. You know Darius.'

She didn't; that was the problem. But one thing she had discovered was where he kept his wretched safe. Simon hadn't been lying after all—it *was* in the study, just very well concealed behind a large oil-painting. Just like a flaming pantomime, thought Kitty with sardonic amusement as she stuck her head around the study door to tell them that lunch was ready and found Simon slamming the safe door shut.

Feeling despondent, she rang Caro up from a payphone that afternoon.

'He's always around!' she wailed. 'Sometimes I don't think he's ever going to leave me with a chance to get at the wretched safe! I don't even know if he really trusts me.'

'He doesn't trust anyone,' said Caro bitterly. 'He's an evil man.'

'Ye-es,' said Kitty, trying not to sound too doubtful. Just what kind of man was he? The kind of man it was impossible not to fancy, no matter what awful things a girl knew about him, she knew *that*. And working for him was having a profound effect on her cardio-vascular system, she knew that too.

Darius had told her that she could order anything she needed by phone from any one of several of Perth's up-market stores where he had accounts. But telephoning through orders, and having some faceless person deliver them, hardly made her working day a barrel of laughs, and so she was delighted to discover a perfect Italian delicatessen within walking distance of his house—admittedly quite a long walk, but she enjoyed the exercise.

The shop sold almost everything she needed: the best olive oil, a dazzling array of breads and meats and fresh pasta. There were huge purple cloves of garlic and bouquet-sized bunches of sweet basil, alongside wicker baskets containing the juiciest, tangiest lemons she had ever seen.

Inside the shop it was dark and cool and dim, and filled with the most wondrous scents. It was run by an Italian couple who had emigrated from Naples over thirty years before and who had worked their socks off to ensure a thriving business—hard work which had paid off, because they now owned a shop in this exclusive suburb.

Within days, Kitty was on first-name terms with Giuseppe and Sophia, and they were laughingly 'teaching' her the rudiments of Italian.

'*L'uva è buona,*' said Sophia, placing a bunch of grapes on the glass-topped counter.

'*L'uva è—buona,*' repeated Kitty obediently.

'*Buona!*'

'*Buona!*'

'*Eccellente!*' And then Giuseppe straightened his back as he looked over Kitty's shoulder to what was obviously another customer.

'*Signor*? Can I help you?'

'I've come to carry the lady's bags,' drawled a deep voice behind her, and Kitty whirled round to find Darius standing there. He had obviously just been jogging. He was wearing a black singlet and silky, rather clingy black shorts which displayed every inch of his tanned and sweat-sheened thighs to perfection. His hair had dried into tiny jet tendrils which surrounded his face. Dear God—he should have carried a government health warning! Her heart pounded. Her swallow was instinctive.

'I haven't finished yet,' she told him.

'I can wait.'

She wanted to tell him not to bother, but she knew enough about him to know that if he'd made up his mind to do something, then that was *it*.

It should have been a simple transaction, but she was all fingers and thumbs, at one point even dropping a twenty-dollar bill on top of a display of salami, and Sophia's knowing smile in the direction of the tall, dark-haired man who stood by the entrance was about as subtle as a brick!

But he took both of the bulging carrier-bags from her, and they walked out into the bright sunshine together.

'Do you do all your shopping there?'

'Most of it. It's as fresh as you'll get anywhere else—and Giuseppe and Sophia make shopping into a learning exercise.'

'So I saw. They seem very fond of you.'

'They've four handsome sons they think the world of. But no daughters,' Kitty explained.

He smiled. 'How's your Italian coming along?'

She made a very Latin little wriggling movement with her shoulders. 'So-so!'

He laughed, and she averted her eyes from the strong, muscular limbs which were swinging alongside her. 'I haven't seen you out running before,' she said quickly.

'I don't, much. But if something isn't going right with the film, it helps clear my mind—see things in a new perspective.'

She nodded thoughtfully. At that moment he seemed so—well, not exactly *normal*, because if there were normal men like him walking around, then it would be very difficult for women to concentrate on anything. But there was a strength and an indescribable aura that surrounded him, something very wholesome as well as sexy. She knew that he didn't smoke, that he drank sparingly—and he certainly wasn't the kind of man to gorge himself on junk food! Allied to that was the fact that he played tennis, ran and swam—all the signs of someone who took care of himself. He was also intelligent, witty and extremely successful in his field.

And it became very difficult to imagine him being the kind of man who would knowingly plagiarise the work of an innocent old lady...

'You're looking very thoughtful,' he observed.

'I was just working out what to give you for supper tonight.' It sounded feeble—it *was* feeble. With that pat reply she had fractured what had sounded like a genuine attempt on his part to be pleasant to her. She saw a dark eyebrow move fractionally upwards, and at that moment, for a reason she couldn't work out, she felt rather ashamed of herself.

As they approached the driveway to his house, a small and very dusty boy popped out from behind the big laurel hedge, and Kitty's heart took a nose-dive. It was Wayne. He sometimes waited for her when she returned from a shopping trip, but this was the first time he'd ever seen Darius.

'G'day, Kitty!' he called.

She decided to brave it out, praying that Wayne wouldn't be his normal garrulous self. 'G'day, Wayne.' She smiled back, echoing the friendly Australian greeting, but she made a frantic little sideways movement with her eyes in Darius's direction.

Wayne apparently didn't notice it. 'Can I come in for cake this afternoon?' he enquired hopefully. 'Please, Kitty?'

Kitty realised that 'our little secret' was about to be exposed, and she turned slightly anxious blue eyes on Darius. 'Um—you don't have any objection to Wayne coming to the house for cake, do you?'

There was only the merest creasing between the two dark wings of his eyebrows. 'Not at all,' he murmured. 'Please feel free.'

'Good. OK, I'll see you later, Wayne—'bout three?'

'*Great*! Thanks, Kitty—see you this arvo!' He disappeared back into the hedge.

Darius stopped beside the ornate, wrought-iron gate while the guard unlocked it. 'Who's Wayne?' he asked, the silver-grey eyes glinting with inquisitive light.

She *wasn't* sorry that she'd asked him—no, siree. 'He lives next door,' she said defensively. 'He's the housekeeper's son.'

'And he doesn't get cake there?'

Her blue eyes sparked. How tight could you get? She should have guessed! 'You can deduct it from my salary if you like.'

He frowned. 'Don't be ridiculous. That isn't what I meant, and you know it.'

'I don't know anything of the sort! He probably doesn't get cake there, actually,' said Kitty angrily. 'He doesn't get a lot, since his mother is virtually employed as a skivvy.' She stared at the long, winding path which led to his enormous house. 'But what would you know about that?' she finished on a bitter note, and made as if to turn away, but he caught her roughly by the arm, his firm grip making her nerve-endings tingle.

'Whereas you, of course, Kitty, are the world expert on poverty, I suppose—with your fancy boarding-schools and finishing-schools—yes, I've read your c.v!'

She met his accusing stare with defiance. 'So? You're in the same boat, aren't you?' she accused. 'You know nothing about poverty either, do you, with all *this*——' she made an all-encompassing gesture with her hands '—at your disposal?'

'You disappoint me,' he said quietly. 'I had credited you with a little more intelligence than to think, just because I have all this now, that it was always so. Are you just so determined to think badly of me, Kitty?' he demanded harshly. 'And tell me, is this an attitude you have towards all men, or is it just me in particular? What made you so cynical about men?' he finished quietly.

She stared at him steadily, but inwardly she was shaken by his accusation. 'How you have the nerve to talk to *me* about cynicism I don't know!' she flared. 'I thought that you invented the word...!' Her words tailed off as she remembered just who she was speaking to, when he astounded her.

'If you must know, Kitty, I probably have more in common with young Wayne than you think. My mother, too, was a "skivvy", as you so nicely put it. After my father died, she worked just about every hour that God sent to make the money to keep me in school. Unfortunately—' and here his face took on a dark, bleak look which was at odds with the almost calm way in which he spoke '—she died before she saw all her hard work come to something. I wasn't,' he said deliberately, 'born with a silver spoon in my mouth. Not like you Kitty.'

She shook her head, wanting to justify what she'd said, wanting him to take that look of barely restrained censure off his face. 'But deprivation is all relative, Darius,' she answered, equally quietly. 'Yes, I came from a wealthy family—I had the wealth that your mother struggled for—but maybe you had a warm, loving home. I certainly didn't. I come from the kind of family where children are packed off to boarding-school at the age of eight, told that the worst crime you could possibly commit is to let your feelings show...' Her voice tailed off as she heard a perilous wobble in it. *Now* what was she doing, pouring her heart out to a man like Darius?

His eyes narrowed in comprehension. 'Tell me about Wayne and his mother,' he said unexpectedly, with a complete change of subject she was grateful for, though it still took her a couple of seconds to get her voice back under control.

'All I know is that she works all hours of the day and night for someone who—from Wayne's description anyway—sounds like a number one spoilt bitch.'

'You sound as though you know my neighbours well,' he said drily.

She had the grace to look shamefaced. 'I haven't met her,' she admitted. 'And I shouldn't have said that—it's just that Wayne seems to live in fear of her. There are about eight million rules for things he isn't allowed to do. He isn't allowed on the patio, and she won't let him swim in the pool. Sometimes——' But she shut her mouth quickly. Oh, hell—now she'd gone and given *that* away too!

'Sometimes?' he prompted.

She thought of the times when she had sneaked Wayne into the pool while Darius had been in his study, or sitting at the big dining-room table in a meeting. 'Well, I've let him use yours once or twice. I've been—er—teaching him how to swim.' She bit her lip anxiously, realising that she'd probably used up her 'last chance'—with interest. 'I shouldn't have done that,' she said quietly.

He frowned. 'It might have been nice to have been asked. Am I really so much of an ogre that you felt you couldn't?'

In theory, yes. He was a powerful man who had ripped off a dear old lady.

But how difficult it was for her to remember that now. In this seeping warm sunshine he was a million light-years away from that image.

She shook her head to try to clear the hold he had on her. She was falling under his spell once more. 'I should have asked you, Darius. I'm sorry.'

'It doesn't matter.' Then, completely unexpectedly, he asked, 'What *kind* of cake?'

She stared at him in confusion. 'What?'

'What kind of cake are you making him?'

If he'd disappeared in a cloud of smoke, she couldn't have been more astonished. 'I thought I'd do chocolate.'

He made a great show of smacking his lips in the time-honoured manner of television commercials. He did it very convincingly and Kitty laughed, suddenly feeling as though she'd drunk a glass of champagne very quickly on an empty stomach.

'Which just happens to be my favourite,' he drawled. 'So if Simon and I should happen along to the kitchen at around three...?'

'Oh, you don't have to do that,' she protested quickly, afraid of pushing her luck. 'I'll bring you a tray——'

He shook his head. 'No, I'd like to chat to Wayne. I don't come into contact much with children.'

Did he sound wistful, thought Kitty, or was she simply imagining it? But he was thirty-two, after all, and presumably at some point he must have thought about having children... She violently pushed the thought away to the back of her head and, without even thinking about it, went to the kitchen where she set about making the most complicated and impressive chocolate cake that it was possible to imagine.

Darius arrived without Simon, and accepted a cup of tea accompanied by a mammoth portion of chocolate cake.

Wayne was unusually quiet, obviously shy at meeting the man who he now realised was Kitty's boss.

'Thought he was yer fella,' he'd hissed loudly as a denim-clad Darius had strolled into the kitchen, and Kitty had darted an anxious glance to see if Darius had heard. But, thank goodness, he hadn't.

But as the spectacular cake became nothing more than a memory and a mountain of crumbs, Wayne gradually relaxed, and by the end of the half-hour the two of them were chatting knowledgeably about Australian Rules football.

Was it Kitty's imagination or did Darius's meeting Wayne mark a turning-point in their relationship? Had he softened?

No, softened was entirely the wrong description for a man who could still be autocratic and demanding.

Less harsh, then, that chilly distance tempered— which brought with it a spate of infinitely more disturbing dreams, and Kitty began to wonder whether she would ever spend an undisturbed night again...

Waking very early one morning after one such fitful night, with the heat of the day already quite intense, Kitty looked at her clock to find that it read just after six, and decided to go for an early-morning swim before making an old-fashioned kedgeree for breakfast.

She slipped on her pale blue swimsuit and walked out into the glorious morning towards the dappled beauty of the pool, marvelling as always as she passed underneath the bright scarlet flowers of a flame-tree.

She was not alone.

For there, cleaving his way through the water, with all the speed and power she had instinctively known he would possess in the water, was Darius.

She stood quietly, hidden by the large leaves of a fragrant shrub, just watching him, feasting her eyes on his magnificent beauty as a starving man would on a banquet.

He swam with style and rhythm, face down in the water, turning to the side for air every third stroke. She watched as each arm swung out through the water in the curving arc of the properly taught swimmer, watched as the muscular thighs powered his sleek, tanned frame through the turquoise clarity of the water.

He had done four lengths in this fashion before, without giving any sign that he was about to do so, he stopped directly in front of where Kitty stood partially concealed, and hauled himself up to lean on his elbows at the side of the pool.

'So why don't you stop spectating and join in?' he drawled.

Kitty felt like some sort of peeping Tom, and when she emerged from behind the shrub her face was as pink as a flamingo's wing.

'I wasn't staring,' she said defiantly.

'No? For someone who wasn't staring, you certainly took your time. Four lengths, by my reckoning.'

Oh! 'How on earth do you know that?' she asked crossly, though crosser still with herself for behaving like some little groupie.

'Kitty,' he said drily, 'you're rather difficult to miss with all that hair. In fact, standing there with the sun behind you, you make a fairly arresting sight. And it's the first time I've ever seen it down,' he added. 'So are you coming in or not? Or are you purely a solo swimmer?

She shook her head, and great handfuls of red hair fell down over the bodice of her pale blue swimsuit. 'I'll swim with you,' she said, trying hard not to croak from a mouth gone strangely dry. Well, she defended herself, it would look rather odd not to, wouldn't it?

She stood by the deep end, poised to dive, suddenly determined to impress him, to show him that she knew something other than how to make a perfect pie-crust. Arms back, head tipped back like a figure-head, she executed a perfect dive, swimming the length before coming up beside him.

He was laughing. 'Show-off!' His grey eyes flashed. 'You're very good.'

'Aren't I?' she said demurely, but there was a challenge in her voice, and he must have heard and accepted it, for wordlessly they turned in unison, racing up the length of the pool. Kitty had beaten men in the water before, but Darius was a far stronger swimmer than anyone else she'd raced against, and not once did she come anywhere close to beating him.

It was heaven—the coolness of the water, the beating of the sun on her head, the visual pleasure of watching the dark-haired man who swam beside her, who was as relaxed as she'd ever seen him.

It was getting late, and she still had breakfast to prepare, and so it seemed crazy not to get out when he did, though she refused his offer of a hand out,

sliding out nimbly before wrapping herself with indecent haste in the luxurious thickness of her
towelling robe, though he sat there in nothing but
his trunks. They sat side by side, dangling their feet
in the pool while they regained their breath.

He was looking at her hair, which was dripping
like limp corkscrews down her back. 'You don't
mind getting your hair wet, then?' he queried.

She looked directly into the curious pewter eyes.
'You don't,' she pointed out.

'But I'm a man.'

She laughed. 'That doesn't deserve a reply.'

He was undeterred. 'Most women tie it up, then
swim with their heads stuck out of the water, like
hens.'

'Hens don't swim.'

He grinned. 'Don't be pernickety. How I imagine they *would* swim, if they could. You don't
mind getting your face wet either.'

'Neither do you.'

'But I'm a man, and *men*,' he emphasised, seeing
her face, 'don't wear mascara.'

'And neither do I.'

'I'd noticed. You don't wear foundation either,
do you? Or lipstick?'

She bristled, her insecurity rearing its appro-
priately ugly head. 'You make it sound——'

'Different. Unusual.'

But plain. 'You sound as though you've never
seen a woman without make-up before,' she said.

'Well, I haven't,' he answered simply. 'Not in the
normal sense, anyway. Women I see through the
cameras wear tons of make-up because they have

to. Other women, well, they wear a lot too, but for different reasons.'

For attracting men like *you*, thought Kitty wistfully, thinking of Janet's perfect vermilion lips, Julia's long, spikily mascaraed eyelashes.

'And, of course, make-up does often pose a slight problem in what it conceals,' he continued. 'Sometimes I've woken up next to a woman who has slipped out some time in the night to wash it all off—and it's like looking into the face of a total strang——'

'*Don't*!' she interrupted hotly, standing up quickly.

'Don't what?' he asked as he stood up beside her.

'I *don't* want to hear about your love-life!'

'Oh?' he asked innocently, but he was grinning. 'And why's that?'

'Because I don't!' she retorted, with brainless logic. Because I know that you're an evil man who can steal an old woman's ideas without compunction—that *should* have been the reason why the idea repulsed her, but it was not. It was because a stupid, deep, painful shard of jealousy had lanced at her heart. Oh, Kitty, she thought helplessly. Just what are you getting into here?

'I'm going in,' she announced flatly, but he stayed her with a look.

'A swim with you in the morning's probably equivalent to an hour in the gym—perhaps we should make a habit of it,' he remarked. 'This followed by contentious and lively debate—and now you're off to make me one of your delectable meals.

Do you know . . . a man could get quite used to this kind of treatment, Kitty?'

And because so, too, could a woman—especially *this* woman—she snapped at him, 'It sounds as though you need a wife, Darius!'

There was an odd silence, and Kitty could have curled up and died at the thought of how this disgustingly inflated ego would choose to interpret *that* remark. 'I'd better go and start breakfast,' she said, eager to escape.

But he, it seemed, had all the time in the world.

'Did you always want to be a cook?' he asked curiously.

She glared, immediately defensive. She had grown tired of the dismissive way that cooking was treated by the public at large. 'The implication being that it's a somehow unworthy profession?'

'Whoa!' He raised his hands in defence. 'I didn't say that.'

'It's what most people think.'

'But not you?'

'I think it's art.'

'Art?' He sounded surprised.

'Yes, art,' she said, a trifle crossly, warming to one of her favourite subjects. 'Edible art. Juxtaposing different colours and textures and flavours.'

'Only to be gobbled up, though?' He sounded amused.

'Ah! But that's what makes it unique,' she argued. 'Because all you have left are the memories. A little like spring flowers—much more evocative because they're so brief—just like every culinary experience.' Oh, dear—now she probably sounded completely over the top.

But he was staring at her. 'Such passion,' he observed, then said something altogether surprising. 'You know, if you really do feel so enthusiastic about the composition of food, then perhaps you might be good at styling it, for films.'

She blinked. 'What's styling?'

He shrugged those broad, muscular shoulders, sending little rivulets of water on a slow, delectable route down his back. 'Think how many scenes in films involve food,' he said. 'An intimate dinner for two. A child's birthday. A large wedding. And think about how different a medieval banquet would be from a meal in a wartime film set in the forties. Do you know anything about the history of food?'

'A little.'

'Learn more,' he suggested. 'You might want to think about changing direction some time.'

She allowed herself one brief fantasy of working alongside Darius, of styling for his films, before ruthlessly dismissing it. She raked her fingers back through her hair to dry it, knowing that she really ought to be getting back, yet unwilling to leave him when he was in this sort of glorious mood.

He picked up a towel and rubbed it over his hair. 'Did you do anything else—before you started cooking?'

She shook her head, surprised that he was remotely interested. 'No. I wasn't really qualified to do anything else. The school my mother sent me to concentrated on turning out "ladies" rather than scholars. So we were encouraged to excel at cooking, flower-arranging, needlework, deportment, except...' She faltered. Why on *earth* was she telling him all this?

'Except?'

She bit her lip, embarrassed at having given so much away. 'Oh, nothing.'

But he took no notice whatsoever of her reluctance to continue. 'So why weren't you any good at deportment?' he persisted.

'It wasn't that I wasn't any good...'

'What was it, then?'

'It was my mother's old school—she was their star pupil in her time. She had all the qualities they held dear—grace, elegance, beauty—whereas I was just...' She stopped, furious with herself for drawing attention to her faults, but to her surprise he wasn't laughing at her. He had narrowed his eyes, as though viewing her with dispassionately critical eyes.

'You have exceptionally beautiful hair,' he remarked. 'Almost Pre-Raphaelite. I can count at least twenty different shades of red in it. Why don't you wear it down more often?'

'Because I can't do a thing with it, as they say.' She gave a little grimace, knowing that the cliché would probably grate, but she couldn't think of anything more original to say—she was too busy trying not to blink with incredulous delight. Her hair had been described as 'ginger-nob' at school— *never* as 'exceptionally beautiful'.

Again, an oddly uncomfortable silence descended on them. 'What's for breakfast?' he asked eventually.

That brought her right back down to earth. 'Kedgeree,' she said briskly. And then, to put things back on a more formal footing, 'I hope you like it?'

'I love it—though I've only ever eaten it in restaurants.'

She remembered every Saturday morning of the summer holidays as a child, when the yellowy mixture of fish and rice and eggs would be served in a great old-fashioned silver salver and left on the hotplate on top of the old-fashioned sideboard. 'Never at home?' she quizzed. 'Didn't your mother ever make it for you?'

For a moment, the silver eyes shadowed. 'My mother didn't have a lot of time for cooking,' he said rather bitterly, and Kitty remembered he'd told her how hard his mother had worked, and could have kicked herself for asking.

He must have seen the look, for he glowered at her. 'I'll see you at breakfast,' he said darkly, and off he went, his broad shoulders set and tight, leaving Kitty with feelings of anger and unwilling longing, and an overriding confusion and surprise at what had just taken place.

CHAPTER SEVEN

To Kitty's surprise Darius started dropping into the kitchen most days, and afternoon tea with Wayne became something of a ritual. Once or twice he even arrived ages before Wayne was due, and he would sit down at the kitchen table, scribbling notes into the fat black notepad he always carried with him, sipping the tea she made him. Once she surprised him sitting staring at her with such an odd expression on his face that she blurted the question out without thinking. 'Is something wrong?'

He shook his head. 'I was just thinking that there's something rather comfortable about sitting in a kitchen with all your baking spicing the air.'

She could have sworn that she heard a touch of wistfulness in his voice. 'I know what you mean. Sort of—heart of the house and all that?'

'Yeah. Something like that.' And he picked up his pen and began to write.

Kitty carried on beating in silence. None of this was turning out how she'd expected. She wasn't supposed to be swapping confidences with him. Feeling at ease with him.

And Wayne worshipped the ground that Darius walked on. It quickly became obvious to her that Darius was one of those people who were naturally very good with children. He didn't talk down to them. Conversely, he didn't patronise Wayne by being man-to-man with him. And Wayne, who had never had a father-figure in his life, quite simply adored him.

Wayne's mother was housekeeper to one Anna-Maria Rawlings, and, according to Wayne, the only thing in Mrs Rawlings's favour was that several months earlier she had consented to let him have a kitten of his own, ostensibly to keep the mice away, but in reality the animal provided a much loved playmate for the lonely little boy, growing up in isolation from his peers in the splendid and ornate fortress which happened to be his 'home' only by chance.

'She's divorced,' Wayne declared in answer to an innocent question from Kitty one day, his mouth full of cherry scone.

'You're dropping crumbs everywhere,' said Kitty automatically as she poured out tea.

'An' her favourite hobby is watching you play tennis!' he told Darius sagely.

Kitty dreaded to think what would come next—Wayne was well-known for his plain speaking. 'More cake, Wayne?' she asked hopefully, praying that he'd drop the subject.

He didn't. 'Yeah—she thinks you're the business! Heard her talking to some of her friends about it—apparently you've got the sexiest bum in Western Australia!'

'That's *enough*, Wayne!' interjected Kitty sternly as she glanced over in Darius's direction to see how the subject of so much female speculation was responding. He looked, she thought, very mildly amused, nothing more. But then, it probably happened several times a day...

In this curious state of suspension, Kitty muddled along, wishing that he would take one of the trips away he'd spoken about which would leave her alone in the house. Sometimes it was hard to believe why she really was here—it all seemed so farfetched. And she was finding it daily more difficult to imagine Darius in his role as blackguard. In fact, she began rather desperately wishing that this whole idea of Caro's really *were* a figment of her imagination. So that even while she prayed for Darius to go away on business part of her was dreading having to break into his safe. And, if she was perfectly honest with herself, dreading even more having to leave...

She was busy making a mango sorbet one morning when the kitchen door was flung open, and Wayne stumbled in, his face as white as chalk, his mouth trembling like a leaf.

'Kitty! Quick!'

She dropped her spoon with a clatter and rushed to the boy's side. 'What on earth's the matter?' she demanded. 'What is it?'

'It's—it's—Mersey,' he stuttered, mentioning the name of his cat.

'What's the matter with him?'

Wayne had gone a sort of pale green colour. 'He's been run over—by the gate. I don't think he's alive. I ran in to tell Mrs Rawlings——' his voice broke on a sob '—and she just told me that she was busy and she didn't want to know. Kitty, *please* . . . can *you* do something?'

Kitty put her arms round him. 'Well, we need to call the vet, obviously——'

'We can't. *She's* refused to pay. And Mum can't afford to.'

'Oh, God.' Kitty thought quickly. 'You go and stay with Mersey. I'll ask Darius.'

She burst into the dining-room where ten people sat round the table, Darius at the head. They all looked up, and she realised what a sight she must look—she hadn't even washed her sticky, mango-covered hands.

He took one look at her face and got to his feet. 'What is it?' he asked quickly. 'What's happened?'

'It's Mersey—Wayne's cat,' she elucidated. 'It's been run over outside.'

'Kitty—what can *I* do? You need a vet——'

'But Mrs Rawlings is refusing to pay. Wayne's mother can't afford to—and they think the cat's *dying* . . .' Her voice broke, just a little, and Darius came round to her side immediately.

'Carry on talking about the scene in the light air-craft,' he said abruptly. 'Simon—get hold of the best available veterinary surgeon and ask him to bill me. Come and show me, Kitty.'

Outside, Mersey was a sad and mangled mass of blood-soaked fur, and was mewing pitifully. Tears from Wayne's eyes were dripping down, and Darius moved him gently aside and looked over the animal. 'I think it's probably not as bad as it looks. Just keep talking to him, old son—he knows your voice, doesn't he?'

Wayne nodded, too choked with emotion to speak.

'Well, then—keep talking.'

The vet's ambulance arrived, and the cat was rushed away. Kitty kept Wayne in the kitchen with her, making him help her bake another cake in an effort to keep his mind off things, and two hours later word came back from the vet that Mersey would live, but that he would have to have one of his legs amputated.

'All's well,' said Kitty tiredly, after she'd provided lunch for ten and packed an emotional but no longer crying Wayne back home.

But all was not well, because a day later Wayne was back in a similar state of distress and at first Kitty thought that the cat had died.

'It's worse than that,' he said in a small voice which shook. 'She says that I can't have the cat back. Says that she isn't having a deformed animal living in *her* house. And the vet says that the chances of someone buying a three-legged cat are zilch—Mersey'll have to be put down,' he sobbed.

Darius, who had obviously been alerted by the sound of Wayne's crying, stood in the kitchen doorway and said something soft and very explicit under his breath. He walked over to Wayne and put one hand on the boy's shoulder. 'Don't worry,' he said comfortingly. 'I'll sort this out.'

At six o'clock that evening, Kitty was busy making Yorkshire pudding when Simon's head appeared round the kitchen door. 'Guess who's coming to dinner?'

Kitty's hand carried on beating. She had just insisted that Wayne go back home to his mother. 'It's a film, starring Sidney Poitier,' she replied, poker-faced.

'Ha ha! Very funny.' He came in. 'Aren't you interested?'

'Why should I be?' She carried on beating, trying to concentrate on making the whip of the fork against the batter sound like horses' hooves clip-clopping over cobblestones, as her old cookery teacher used to tell her. And not on who Darius was eating with. It was probably Julia. *Again.* She'd eaten with him three times last week. Not that she was counting. 'So who *is* coming for dinner?' she asked casually, unable to stifle her inquisitiveness any longer.

'The infamous Mrs Rawlings—young Mersey's persecutor.'

'*Really*?'

'Really.'

'I wonder why?'

Simon shrugged. 'I should think that Darius has decided to use charm where all else has failed.'

The idea of this disturbed her. And what did this application of charm consist of? A session in bed with 'the sexiest bum in Western Australia'? Kitty shuddered. This was Darius being manipulative, and that image smacked too much of the Darius who had cheated Caro. It was an image she had foolishly been trying to push to the back of her mind because it conflicted too much with the man she had grown to know—the one who cared about small boys and disabled cats...

'So no arsenic in the gravy, huh, Kitty?' laughed Simon, but he stopped when he saw her tight expression.

At seven-thirty Kitty heard the peal of the front doorbell, followed by the rumble of Darius's deep voice interspersed with the lighter, trilling tones of female laughter.

Kitty didn't know what she had expected Anna-Maria Rawlings to look like—but she certainly got a shock!

When Wayne had described his mother's boss as 'old Ma Rawlings', Kitty had conjured up a mental picture of a middle-aged old-school harridan, ruling the house with a rod of iron. But as Kitty clattered over to the table with a tray she saw that the reality was something else.

Anna-Maria Rawlings was aged about thirty-five, and was all large, lustrous eyes and full, sensuous lips. She had a blunt-cut bob in the classic style, as dark and as shiny as a raven's wing, which fell to her perfectly carved jaw. With her kohl-outlined dark eyes and dark red mouth, she looked like Cleopatra, a look which was emphasised by the draped white silk dress she wore, knee-length and very simple, but so exquisitely cut that it clung to every perfect and slender curve. Kitty felt like a construction worker in the blue overall which covered her rust-coloured Bermudas and cream T-shirt.

'Mrs Rawlings——' began Darius.

'Anna-Maria, *please*!' she interrupted smilingly.

'Meet Kitty Goodman—she works as my chef.'

'Hello,' said Kitty, wiping a hand down the front of her overall—not that it was a dirty hand; it was just the effect the woman was having on her! She held it out.

Anna-Maria took it briefly, as though she had been offered the poisoned chalice. 'How do you do?' she asked, in a voice of pure ice-cubes. 'So you're the girl who is responsible for that wretched cat.'

Kitty blinked. 'Sorry?'

'Kitty helped save the cat's life,' Darius pointed out.

A rueful little smile was darted at him, but Kitty got the full impact of a chilly stare. 'I'm sure you were well-intentioned, but *really*! The animal was in the most *appalling* condition—it really shouldn't have been allowed to live.'

Kitty's eyes widened in astonishment. 'But Wayne loves that cat,' she protested.

'*He* may love it, *I* do not—and it happens to be *my* house.'

Kitty opened her mouth.

'Now, now,' interjected Darius peaceably. 'I'm sure that there's a way to solve this amicably.'

'There is,' smiled Anna-Maria, with all the sincerity of a politician. 'I've told Wayne that the cat will have to go.'

Kitty shot her a furious look, and she didn't care whether it was bad manners or not as she deliberately crashed unceremoniously out of the door, because if she'd stayed, there was no saying *what* she might have done. Dolloped a ladle of hot soup all

over Anna-Maria Rawlings's beautiful white silk
dress perhaps!

She managed to keep her face composed as she
flitted in and out, but did not dare to look at Darius
for fear that he would see the mutiny sparking in
her eyes, although she could sense that he watched
her. She could feel his gaze on her all the time as
she brought in plates and dishes. Well, *that* would
irritate Mrs Rawlings! She felt that it was no co-
incidence that, each time she entered the room,
Anna-Maria would start speaking in a loud and
somewhat imperious voice, deliberately, Kitty felt,
emphasising the social divide between she who
waited and they who dined.

Who cares? thought Kitty defiantly as she placed
the steaming dishes on the table, glad that she had
cooked roast beef accompanied by what the reed-
like Anna-Maria probably thought were stodgy ac-
companiments of cauliflower cheese and roast po-
tatoes. No doubt she would pick delicately at the
contents of her plate. Well, you won't impress
Darius like that, thought Kitty with malicious glee—
Darius is the kind of man who likes to see food
appreciated, and enjoyed.

And then she brought herself up short. What was
happening to her? She'd been here less than a
month and yet here she was, concocting fantasies.
Who was this man she imagined she knew so well?
If what Caro said was true, then she really didn't
know him at all.

If what Caro said was true.

She shook her head. Of course it was true. Why
on earth would Caro lie about something like that?

Perhaps she wasn't altogether surprised when Darius stayed her with a hand put lightly over her arm as she placed his coffee-cup in front of him. 'Stay and join us for coffee, Kitty. Or perhaps you'd care for wine?'

'Yes, do,' interjected Anna-Maria patronisingly. 'Take off your overall and sit down.'

Kitty's lips gave a little amused upward twist. 'Oh, no, really,' she said in a solemn voice. 'Really, I couldn't.'

Back in the kitchen, she scrubbed furiously at the dirty saucepans, pausing only when she heard voices in the hall. Unable to stop herself, she crept over to the slightly open door, to see Darius and Anna-Maria alone in the hall, her starkly beautiful profile held up to stare at him.

'Oh, *Darius*,' she pouted. 'The owner of the club's a personal friend of mine—and they do the best cocktails in the whole state. Come on—you can't be *that* tired.' And a hand moved up to trickle seductively down his chest, and to lie possessively over his heart. 'And besides, I have certain fool-proof methods of revitalisation...'

Her voice trailed off, and Kitty couldn't make out his amused reply. She felt sick, angry with herself for ever having agreed to get involved with such a house, and such a man—and even angrier with the horrifyingly vivid images she was conjuring up, of Darius making love to the beautiful and exotic Anna-Maria, erotic images which scorched themselves into her unwilling brain, filling her heart with a blackly jealous rage. And jealous is the last thing I want to feel, she thought desperately...

'Why on earth did you scuttle off like that?' came a deep voice from the doorway. 'I meant it when I said I'd like you to join us. I thought you'd welcome the chance to wax lyrical about Mersey, and plead his case for him.'

The deep voice shocked her out of her disturbing thoughts, and she whirled round to find him standing there, very still, just watching her. Still trying to rid herself of the unreasonable anger that Anna-Maria's behaviour with him had evoked, she was unaware that the scouring-pad which she held was dripping soapy water all over the tiled floor.

He took the pad from her and replaced it in the sink.

'Why,' he repeated, 'didn't you join us for coffee? I could have done with a little light relief.'

'Because I don't like to be patronised, that's why.'

His eyes narrowed fractionally. 'Mrs Rawlings was very rude to you. I'm sorry.'

'Anna-Maria,' corrected Kitty sarcastically. 'Of *course* she was rude to me,' she bit out angrily before she could stop herself. 'It was perfectly obvious how she hoped to spend the evening with you—and then you ruined it all by trying to get your cook to join you!'

'You surely aren't suggesting that I was going to end the evening with the poisonous Anna-Maria in my bed?' he murmured.

'Of course not,' she said stiffly, unused to such frankness. 'Julia wouldn't like it, would she?' Fish, fish, fish!

'Julia isn't my lover,' he said thoughtfully.

'Oh?' She stared at him disbelievingly, and then, before she could stop herself, demanded, 'Well, what about Janet?'

An angry glint lit the silver eyes. '*Janet*? I do not date twenty-year-olds, Kitty. In fact, I'm not seeing anyone right now.' His voice darkened. 'Why? Would it bother you if I was?'

'No, it would not!' she lied.

'I don't believe you,' he murmured. 'Not a word.'

Her eyes widened in shock. 'What do you mean?' she whispered, taking his words at face value.

'Just that you fascinate me, Kitty. You blow hot, then cold. One minute those blue eyes are flashing fire, sending me a message that sends my blood-pressure soaring, the next they're wide and frightened.'

Kitty felt a pulse beating wildly at her temple. She fought for control; she thought of Caro, but nothing seemed to work. The pulse was refusing to take heed of the voice of reason. Even silently saying Caro's name over and over again, like a talisman which should by rights have protected her from the potency of his presence, in fact did absolutely nothing to prevent the rush of terrifying excitement which flooded over her as he took a step closer.

'All evening I've been watching you. You knew that, didn't you? I couldn't keep my eyes off you. You move so gracefully, Kitty. Like some pale wraith, some fey fantasy-figure I've conjured up. I kept imagining that if I looked away for a moment you might just disappear.'

She was breathless, stunned by his words, by the vision of her that they had created, too stunned to do more than stare up at him, wanting him to keep speaking to her in that incredibly seductive manner forcver.

'Do you know that your eyes——' his voice had dropped to a husky whisper '—are the most beautiful blue I've ever seen in my life?'

She drew in a breath as he lifted his hand to touch her hair, neatly confined by its blue velvet ribbon.

'And your skin is as pale as mayonnaise,' he continued, a small smile playing around his lips as he took in her parted lips, the fluttering pulse just where the tangle of curls was pushed back.

'So good,' he whispered, and bent his head so that she could feel his warm breath on her face. 'Good enough to eat, aren't you, Kitty?'

The analogy was so unexpected, and so appropriate, that she felt dizzy with longing as he put his arms around her shoulders and she closed her eyes with sheer, helpless pleasure as he bent his head to kiss her.

And what a kiss.

If the first time he'd kissed her had knocked her for six, then this knocked her for sixty. It was like being hit off balance by a bolt of electricity. His mouth covered hers almost roughly, with a hard, delectable pressure, but his hands didn't touch her body, much as she wanted them to. His very restraint seemed to inflame her, so that it was she who slipped her still soapy damp arms around his waist, clinging on to him so that his hard body was held tightly against hers.

She felt his body spring into urgent life as they made contact, and, although her inexperience should have made her intimidated by such an intimate display of his size and his power, it did no such thing. Instead, the sensation of him, so hard and aroused, thrilled her to the very core and she made a little sound of assent in the back of her throat.

She heard his own sigh as his hands came down, sweetly capturing the small mounds of her breasts, his fingers teasing and tantalising the tips into two deliciously, painfully hard nubs which pushed against his hands, sending him a silent, shameless message that her body was screaming for him.

Still kissing her in that deep, sweet way, he moved his hands down to hold her hips, moulding his own into them in a flagrantly sexual movement, which sent her heart racing into overdrive. Still holding her like that, he pushed her back against the draining-board. For a second her eyes flew open, scarcely able to believe that this was happening to her, and then again he moved himself against her in an explicit circle of seductive dance and all her reservations vanished as the sensations he was provoking grew more powerful with each moment that passed. She was becoming lost in some thick mist of desire, lost... Totally lost, was her last sane thought as she reached her fingers up to thread them in the blackness of his hair.

He stopped kissing her for a moment, his breathing very unsteady, two flushed lines of colour on his high cheekbones. A small smile played on his lips as he raised his head to stare down into her face, the mercurial eyes going ruefully to the blue overall which covered her T-shirt.

'Shall we take this off?' he suggested calmly, again brushing his finger over each breast, and she was almost about to raise her arms to be undressed like a compliant child, when the arrogance of his calm assumption at last sank in.

Foolishly, she pushed at the solid wall of his chest, which had absolutely no effect at all, but his hands dropped from her immediately, and a cool question appeared in his eyes.

'Changed your mind?' he enquired idly.

She erupted with fury as she registered that she was still lying back against the draining-board, that... Oh, good heavens, where would it all have ended? If he hadn't been so insolent about undressing her, she might actually have let him take her virginity—in the *kitchen*! 'I hadn't made it up in the first place!' she spat at him.

'No?' His lips curved into a coldly sardonic smile. 'Forgive me, but that's not the message I was getting.'

And his words were so patently true that she couldn't bring herself hypocritically to deny them. Because she *had* wanted him...very badly indeed. She'd led him on, and then...

'Do you always try to seduce your employees like this?' she hissed, redirecting her shame into a bitter accusation. She quickly moved away from the sink, and away from him, as if hoping that, by putting a few feet between them, she might rid herself of this overpowering need to have him make love to her again.

'Try?' He actually laughed, but the sound mocked her. 'Let's not fool ourselves, Kitty. I didn't have to try very hard, did I?'

She fumed silently as she registered the insulting implication, and she felt all the blood drain from her face. No, he hadn't had to try at all hard.

And then his eyes narrowed as he pierced her with a searching look. 'What happened just now?' he asked softly. 'One minute you were——'

'I came to my senses,' she said heatedly. 'I'm not an advocate of casual sex—and we hardly know each other—certainly not well enough for *that* kind of thing!' Oh, what a prude she sounded now.

He laughed, very quietly. 'Playing to the rules, are you, Kitty? How very disappointing. I thought you'd be passionate. Spontaneous.'

She struggled to find an insult of her own. The temptation to confront him about Caro—to tell him that she knew just how much of a rat he was—was overwhelming, but she resisted it, going instead for a general rather than a specific insult. 'I suppose you're just one of those men who find it impossible not to make a pass at any member of the female sex from sixteen to sixty, aren't you?' she said scornfully.

The grey eyes hardened briefly. 'Actually, no, I'm not,' he said, drawing his dark brows together in a gesture of perplexity. 'I don't make love to women every moment of my life. Not so swiftly, nor so uninhibitedly either—at least not for a long time.'

It was just the kind of thing that every woman wanted to hear, and she had to remind herself that he was just saying it, that it was nothing more than sweet talk. He was an experienced man of the world, one who knew that seduction had to be tailored to suit each woman. He had probably seen right through to her almost shameful innocence of the opposite sex, and had decided that the best way to succeed in getting her into bed was to single her out, to make her feel somehow *special*.

And, for a moment there, he had almost succeeded.

He lifted his hands towards her face, but she flinched, afraid that if he touched her again her actions would belie her words.

'Don't touch me,' she ordered breathlessly, and she jerked away from him, holding her palms up defensively.

His eyes narrowed, as though taking in for the first time just what a highly charged emotional state she was in. 'What's the matter, Kitty? Why this appalled reaction?' he asked, his voice a softly mocking taunt. 'Surely a man has tried to make love to you before?'

Not like that, and never with such a devastating effect, she thought, a tide of frustrated longing making her knees weak, and she bit her bottom lip as she waited for the weakness to pass.

Her experience of men had been painfully lacking. She had been packed off at the age of eight to a boarding-school run by nuns, which had given her all the freedom of a federal gaol, so until her mid-teens any brushes with the opposite sex had been kept strictly to a minimum. And she had been singularly unimpressed with those she did meet. Only Hugo had seemed different, at first—claiming to value her for her mind. But it had not been her mind which had caused him to throw her down on the bed that night and try virtually to tear the clothes from her body... She remembered his sneering words as she valiantly fought him off and he'd realised that the only way he was going to succeed in having sex with her would be to use force. 'Frankly, I'd rather get my leg over with your mother—at least she doesn't look as though *she'd* be a frigid bitch.' And he'd stormed out of the room in disgust.

'Frigid bitch'.

How Hugo's words had wounded her at the time—and yet in some strange way they had been nothing more than the confirmation of a lifetime spent growing up in the shadow of an infinitely more beautiful mother...

Coming back to the present, Kitty stared up into Darius's silver-grey eyes, her confusion increasing as she thought about what had just almost taken place.

She had let him touch her, make love to her. She'd read of his reputation, and yet it had made no difference. She had wanted him, *really* wanted him—in a way she had never wanted Hugo, and she hadn't felt the tiniest bit frigid in Darius's arms.

Oh, why did things have to be so complicated? she thought, closing her eyes in desperation, as if by doing that she might be able to make all her troubles go away.

His eyes narrowed as he saw her shaky movement. 'What is it?' he snapped out. 'Kitty— look at me!' His arms snaked out, he caught her against him, and she made as if to tense up, but the movement was not even remotely sexual. He peered down into her face, the silver-grey eyes burning as they raked over her widened eyes and trembling lips. 'You're as white as a ghost,' he observed. 'What the hell's the matter?'

I want to go home, she thought miserably as she shook her head in silent response to his question. Away from this house and this deception. Away from this man who I'm beginning to care for. She started to shake so violently that her teeth began to chatter.

His hands moved up to grip her by the shoulders, and he lowered his face to her level, his gaze boring into her with its intensity. 'Kitty, what in heaven's name is the matter with you?' he demanded again.

In the enchanting prison of his arms, the temptation to tell him was enormous, but how could she tell him that she was becoming dangerously fond of him . . . that his power over her was such that she felt she was losing not just her heart, but her mind and her body and her soul as well? And if she told him that he would run a mile. She shook her head. 'Please, Darius. Let me go.'

He swore with softly restrained savagery beneath his breath. 'For God's sake—if I'd known how you were going to react I wouldn't have laid a finger on you. Now, leave everything. *Everything*! That's an order! Janet will clear everything up in the morning.'

He paused, running his hand down the side of her face, his fingers lingering on the soft skin there, and she had to fight the urge to purr with pleasure because the gentle caress made her feel like a petted cat.

'Can you get to bed yourself, or am I going to have to carry you?'

She pulled away from him, because the thought of being cradled against that hard chest shouldn't fill her with such wild, sweet longing. 'I'm perfectly capable of walking. I don't know what came over me.'

'Nor me,' he said grimly. 'I don't usually behave with all the finesse of a randy soldier home on leave.' By now his face too was carved with the harsh lines of weariness. 'Come on,' he said abruptly. 'I'll show you to your annexe.'

She quickly withdrew from him in fright, afraid that if he touched her again he would be able to seduce her with insulting ease. 'No, don't...' she stumbled, and she could see from the ironic comprehension dawning in the silver-cold eyes that he guessed at her fears immediately.

His mouth curved in distaste as he replied, 'Oh, don't worry, Kitty—the word "force" isn't one that's in my vocabulary.'

She could believe it. For who would need force with even a tenth of his sensuality? She was unable to do anything other than let him escort her to her annexe, during which time he behaved with perfect, if exaggerated dignity.

But once there she realised that there was one problem at least that she *could* try to solve. 'Darius,' she said softly.

His eyes were cautious, but a brief light flared in them. 'What?'

'What are we going to do about the cat?'

He stared at her as if she'd just had a complete brainstorm. 'The cat?'

'Wayne's cat,' she told him, puzzled when he tipped his head back and gave a low, cynical laugh.

'I must be slipping,' he said drily. 'Here was I thinking that you might be regretting your decision as much as I am, but no, a lame duck—or in this case—a lame cat—is giving you more food for thought than my lovemaking.'

And yet, surprisingly, he did not sound angry, the way that Hugo had when she'd turned him down. It was more a kind of wry amusement, as if it had never happened to him before, and perhaps it hadn't—she couldn't imagine many women saying no to him.

'So what about the cat, Kitty? What are we to do about it?'

'Couldn't we keep it?' she asked tentatively. 'Wayne could come in and see it—when it suited you, of course,' she added hastily.

He gave a long sigh. 'Very well, Kitty,' he said at last. 'We'll keep the damned cat. I suppose you won't give me a moment's peace unless I do. It can sleep on my bed—I need *something* to keep me warm at night. But that's *it*—do you understand? No more strays, no more sob-stories. Now get into bed and stop looking at me with those big blue eyes,' he said roughly, 'before I forget myself and kiss you again.' But although his words were harsh his hands were almost gentle as they pushed her through the door.

Kitty stumbled inside, going automatically to stare at her reflection in the mirror. 'Big, blue eyes'. No one had ever said *that* to her before. But apart from that what else had he seen in her pale, freckle-spattered face which had given him that hungry, almost intense look?

And after she'd showered she lay naked beneath the sheet, squirming like mad, her body all strung up with tension, regretting her decision to say no to him more than she'd regretted anything in her whole life.

CHAPTER EIGHT

'Do YOU want to forget what happened last night and carry on?' Darius stood with his back to her, so that Kitty couldn't see his face, looking out over the gardens, which were brilliant with colour in the clear early-morning light.

It was a question Kitty had lain awake for most of the night thinking about. Last night had changed everything. She was beginning to fall for Darius, *really* fall for him, and she simply didn't know what to do about it. Should I stay or should I go? she thought. 'Yes,' she lied, buying time. 'I'd like to forget it ever happened.'

At this he turned round, his eyes questioning as they alighted on her face, which she knew was even paler than usual.

'I half expected to see your bags packed this morning,' he said, his eyebrows raised.

'I couldn't bear to go back to waitressing,' she said lightly, trying to make a joke of it.

'No.' His expression was thoughtful. 'But if you stay...' His face hardened. 'I can't give you any guarantee, Kitty, that I won't try to make love to you again.'

Colour flared into her cheeks at his openness. What a way to put it!

Sex, for her, had been a subject never talked about—just a few confusing things whispered about at boarding-school, until she'd found herself a book to read... 'And what if I don't want you to?' she asked quietly.

'Then you are perfectly safe with me.' He gave her a strange smile. 'But you will, Kitty. You know you will. Sooner or later you will want me to make love to you. And I don't think I'll be able to resist you. I'm just giving you fair warning.'

It was such an arrogant assumption, but what was even worse was that she had an awful suspicion that he might be right!

'Are you always so sure of yourself? Of your effect on women?' she asked acidly.

'I'm sure about you,' he said softly, then, with one of his swift changes of subject, 'I'm auditioning an actress today who has the calorie intake of an ant—can you prepare something she'd like?'

She nodded. He'd switched from the subject of how he was going to seduce her to what he wanted for lunch—just like that. He could do it. And somehow she didn't think that *she* could. And in that instant she came to a decision. 'I'll do some salad,' she said steadily, but her voice sounded strained. 'But after lunch I'd like to go out. And I'd like to use one of your cars.'

She saw his eyes narrow. 'To do what?'

She let her lashes flutter down over her eyes. Lying wasn't easy with a pair of perceptive grey eyes staring at her shrewdly. 'Oh, you know—just this and that. I just want to get out and about a bit more,' she mumbled feebly, furious at the stack of clichés which tripped off her tongue. 'I feel a little out of touch up here.'

'Out of touch?' he frowned, still watching her very closely. 'But I thought you told me you didn't have any friends in WA.'

Heavens, he was so sharp she was surprised he didn't cut himself! 'I don't,' she said, the fearful leap in her stomach belying her nonchalance. 'But there are shops, parks. And you're sounding a little like a gaoler, Darius.'

'Forgive me,' he said in a chilly voice. 'Of course you must take one of the cars. Have the Mercedes— it's automatic, and probably the easiest to drive. Here.' He threw her the car keys and she caught them. 'Take as long as you like—the tank's full.'

'I'll be back in time to cook supper,' she said, but he shook his head.

'Don't bother,' he said, but his voice sounded constrained. 'I'll make myself a sandwich.'

After providing lunch for the actress—who looked as though a puff of wind would topple her—Kitty climbed into the open-topped silver car. She managed to get it started first time without any trouble, but her heart pumped erratically as she drove away from the impressive suburb, her mind so busy ticking over that she failed to notice the low black Porsche in her rear mirror as it followed her with all the stealth of a panther.

She had made her mind up. She was going to have to see Caro and tell her that the deal was off. She couldn't go through with it. Not any more. It was too risky. Like playing with fire.

And she was frightened, too. Yes, Darius could be sweet with Wayne, and almost convincingly tender while he was trying to make love to her, but Kitty didn't underestimate for a moment the dark core of steely strength inside the man. Just imagine how he'd be if he discovered that she was intending to rob him! She shivered.

And, besides all that, her whole plan was far more fraught than she or Caro had ever anticipated. Because none of it was happening the way she had thought it would... Yes, he was arrogant, and yes, he had an ego big enough to fill a football stadium, quite apart from what he had done to Caro. But none of that seemed to stop her from fancying him like mad. And the sooner she was out of there the better.

Kitty pushed her foot down experimentally on the accelerator and the car whizzed forward, so that the wind whipped her hair into a frenzy.

She'd never driven a sports car before. Her mother was pretty well off, but she upheld the boring middle-class view that wealth shouldn't be at all ostentatious. Cars were solid, well-built, worthy. This, on the other hand, was—fun! She couldn't help noticing that a lot of other people obviously thought so too, since the zippy little car drew a lot of admiring glances, and she was slightly worried about where to leave it. Supposing someone scratched it? Or stole it?

But Darius would be bound to be insured—and anyway she had far more important things to worry about than his wretched car!

Even so, with sweat trickling down her back, she laboriously hauled up the soft top of the car and fastened it, and walked the short distance to the employment agency which Caro owned. Caro's Kitchen Cookies was situated at one end of Adelaide Terrace in a single office on the ground floor of a small block.

Kitty pushed the door open to hear a telephone trilling.

Although its proprietor looked so eccentric, Caro's Kitchen Cookies had a surprisingly good reputation in the city. It was an old established company, for one thing, and Caro had a certain idiosyncratic charm.

As Kitty walked in, she found Caro wearing some kind of gold and black caftan, her trainer-clad feet lying up on the desk, smoking a foul-smelling cheroot. Still, she wasn't bad for someone of almost sixty-five, thought Kitty, coughing a little as a thick cloud of smoke wafted in her direction.

'Don't like the smoke? No worries!' Caro stubbed the cheroot out in a saucer with a flourish. 'Sit down and tell me your name, dear!'

'It's *me*, Caro—Kitty Goodman,' said Kitty patiently. 'I'm working for Darius Speed. Remember?'

Caro paled, picked up her discarded cheroot and immediately re-lit it. 'Don't!' she shuddered. 'Isn't he a swine?' Before Kitty could answer, she brightened. 'Have you done it yet? Got my script back for me?'

This was the hard part. How to tell Caro that she was no nearer to getting it than she'd been a month ago. That she was stupidly, perilously in danger of falling for the man. Well, there wasn't an easy way to say what she had to.

'Caro—I just don't think I can do it,' she blurted out. 'The safe's in his study; he's always in it, and he doesn't show the slightest inclination to go away—not now *or* in the future. And, apart from the first night I arrived, he's spent every damned evening at home.' And if I stay I'm bound to end up in his bed, and, much as I think I want to, I really *don't* want to do that. 'There it is, Caro. I'm sorry—but I can't.'

Perhaps if Caro had begged, pleaded...or turned on her, been angry... But she said nothing. She just sat there staring into space, her rheumy eyes looking suspiciously misty, and Kitty saw an old woman whose dreams had been sacrificed on the altar of a ruthless man's ambition. And as her heart softened towards Caro it simultaneously hardened towards Darius.

What was she thinking of—wanting to back out now? Where was her grit, her resolve, her determination? Was she prepared to stand back while rich, successful men walked all over little old ladies? No, she was not!

Pushing back her chair, she went over to Caro and put her arm round her shoulders to give her an impulsive hug. 'Don't worry about it, Caro,' she said confidently. 'I'll think of something.'

But her confidence underwent a swift evaporation as she walked out into the bright sunshine again. Just what had she in mind exactly? she wondered as she set off towards the car.

She was so caught up in her maze of confused thoughts that she didn't see the tall, dark-haired man on the opposite side of the road. It was only when a deep and familiar voice spoke in her ear that she jumped out of her skin.

'Hello, Kitty,' he drawled. 'Doing a spot of job-hunting? I thought you told me this morning that you were staying?'

Darius stood mere feet away, silver-grey eyes narrowed. Was that to shield them from the bright sunshine, or were they narrowed in suspicion? she wondered. White-faced, she stared up at him, her worst fears confirmed. 'What—what are you talking about?' she stammered nervously.

A cold smile lifted the corner of his mouth as he nodded in the direction of the building from which she'd just emerged. 'Have you changed your mind about working for me? Because I assume that the reason you're coming out of the employment agency is because you've been looking for another job.'

She let the sigh of relief come out slowly, so slowly that he would think it just a normal breath. 'No. No, I haven't. I just called in to let them know how I'm getting on. You know. They like to hear.'

The silvery eyes blazed, but only for an instant, before resuming a coolly impassive look. 'Do they?' he queried.

'Yes, of course they do!' she agreed eagerly.

'I wish I knew what was going on in that head of yours,' he said blandly. 'I'm usually pretty perceptive about people, but you, Kitty, remain something of an enigma.'

Oh, lord—he *did* suspect! She went on the attack. 'Were you following me?' she demanded.

'Now why should I do that?'

'I—just wondered what you were doing in town.'

'Why shouldn't I be in town? *Now* who's sounding like a gaoler? As a matter of fact, I have a meeting in a few minutes' time.'

And he was out of the house! The safe was unguarded! 'I think I'll go back to the house,' she said casually.

His eyes glinted. 'Yes, do,' he said coolly. 'But please don't disturb Simon, will you? I've left him enough work to keep him busy for hours.'

CHAPTER NINE

DARIUS was strangely quiet all through dinner that evening, and the following morning he walked into the kitchen, his face tight and set. 'Get ready to go out, Kitty; we'll be leaving in half an hour.'

'Leaving?' she asked blankly. 'To go where?'

'We're going to Rottnest Island.'

Rottnest Island.

Kitty had heard of the small island in the Indian Ocean which lay just off the coast, close to Fremantle. And what did he mean—'we' were going to Rottnest? 'Who's going?'

'You and me.'

She swallowed nervously. 'Why?'

He gave her a strange smile. 'I told you—I've been commissioned to do a documentary on the place. I want to go and find myself a location or two.'

'But why do you need me?'

'Because a man needs sustenance—and the food on offer over there is pretty basic. I thought that you could pack a picnic. Have you been there before?'

She shook her head. 'No.'

'Well, there's another reason for going. And this will be your last chance to demonstrate your culinary talents for a while.'

She looked up quickly. Was he *sacking* her? 'What do you mean?'

'I'm planning to fly up to Mount Tom Price on business on our return. So you'll be free to do as you please until I get back. How does that suit you?'

Her heart gave a great leap of excitement. That meant he'd be leaving her alone in the house! At last! Alone, with his safe! He couldn't suspect, after all. She kept her face deliberately neutral. He mustn't guess just how delighted she felt. Instead she continued to sound doubtful about the proposed trip to Rottnest—which she was! 'And how long will we be staying there?'

'A few hours, that's all.'

'Oh.' Well, it sounded safe enough.

'What's the matter, Kitty—afraid to trust yourself alone with me?'

That was precisely what she *was* worried about. He had told her that he couldn't guarantee not making a pass at her again. He had also told her that he was sure that, sooner or later, she would succumb.

Well I won't! she vowed silently.

His eyes glittered like base metal. 'No need to ask what you were thinking then,' he mocked. 'Go and get a waterproof jacket.'

'How are we getting there?'

'I'm sailing us.'

It was impossibly beautiful. *Beautiful*, thought Kitty as she stood on deck and the wind tugged and tugged in a vain effort to free the hair which she'd tied back in its habitual plait. The sea all around them was a wonderful blend of blues—turquoise, aquamarine, and lapis, every blue imaginable and a few more besides. The sunlight bounced off the waves, throwing bright light all over them, so that it bathed the intent figure at the helm with dazzling rays.

It was the first time she'd ever sailed, and already she loved it. Darius had made her put a life-jacket on and she'd applied masses of sunblock, and was spending the journey watching silver fish leaping from the water and strange birds flashing past them in the sunlight.

He turned his head to look at her, and the sight of him, wind-swept and gorgeous as he controlled the large and elegant vessel, in a snowy white T-shirt tucked into clinging denim cut-offs, made her insides turn to water, and she forced herself to look away, grateful that very soon she would be through with this whole business. Thank heavens she wouldn't have to keep up this charade for much longer. When Mr Darius Speed returned from Tom Price—wherever that was—he would find his chef long departed. She forced the interested smile of the eager tourist on to her face. 'Is it very basic on the island?'

'Very.' His teeth were brilliantly white against his tanned skin. 'No cars allowed, so therefore very little pollution. A couple of hotels—and some private houses for rent, too. There are one or two shops which sell provisions. If we hadn't brought a picnic, we could have gone native. I could have caught a fish—cooked it on an open fire. Best food in the world.'

She swallowed. He was managing to make it sound like a paradise she'd have given her eye-teeth to share with him.

She turned her back and stared out at the horizon as he steered the yacht towards the small hump of land which had just appeared.

'How do we get around the island,' she asked, 'if we aren't allowed cars on it?'

'We hire a couple of bikes.'

She couldn't quell the feeling of intense excitement which welled up in her after they'd docked the boat and hired their bicycles. They rode along, sometimes with one of them ahead, sometimes abreast, the wind blowing through their hair, and the only thing she could think of was how much she wanted him. She gave a little shiver even as the warm sun beat down on her bare arms.

From time to time Darius would shout over to her that he wanted to stop, and when this happened Kitty would sit cross-legged on the sand, watching him from behind her sunglasses while he wrote copious notes in a small book, and shot off a few pictures.

This had happened about four times, and Kitty's stomach was beginning to feel extremely empty—in fact she was just sneaking a surreptitious glance at her watch—when his words broke into her thoughts.

'Hungry?'

'Starving.' Or rather she had been, but the sight of those bunched, muscular thighs in the sawn-off

denims was enough to make her thoughts of food
seem suddenly very insignificant indeed... She tried
to concentrate on his nastier aspects, to picture
Caro's sad old face, but her imagination stubbornly refused to work for her—the sun was too
bright, the air too clean, too fresh—and Darius
himself looked too much like a god who'd swooped
down to earth for an afternoon for her to do anything but accept the dull thumping of her heart
which came louder and faster by the second.

She scooped up a handful of the fine sand and
let it trickle between her fingers.

'Let's go and eat,' he murmured. 'I'm working
up quite an appetite.'

She saw innuendo where none was intended, and
knew that she blushed scarlet, and hoped to
goodness he didn't see it as he picked up her bike
and handed it to her.

'Shall we?'

Something in the flash of his eyes as he asked
the question set up a clamorous reaction inside her.
'That would be nice. Where?'

'The island is littered with deserted beaches—let's
just find the prettiest bay to hand.'

Said the spider to the fly, she thought as he gave
her a smile which didn't quite reach his eyes and
she felt tiny goose-bumps spring into life on her
upper arms. He *knows*, she thought, quite
spontaneously.

He *can't* do.

And on the ride to the bay Kitty managed to con-
vince herself that her fears were a case of imagination gone crazily out of control.

The second bay they found was exquisite—a great sweep of a blindingly bright crescent, with the lapping of clear, turquoise waves licking at the soft white sand the only sound to be heard in a world that seemed suddenly empty.

Darius took the cool-box from the basket, put it in the shade of a rock, and began tugging at the zip of his denim cut-offs.

Kitty stared. It looked like every woman's favourite fantasy and her heart leapt erratically, so that his next words came as a complete shock.

'Let's swim before lunch, shall we?' he suggested casually.

Of course. He wanted to swim. What else? Had she for one bizarre moment thought that he was undressing in order to leap on her?

But join him? Splash around half-naked in the sea with him? Kitty was horrified at the direction her thoughts had taken, and, already feeling vulnerable and exposed enough in this sheltered paradise, shook her head. 'I won't, thanks.'

'Oh, come on,' he said softly. 'It's beautiful.'

By now he had stripped off to reveal a tanned and hard-packed muscular body clad in longish swimming-trunks which *should* have been decent, but which, when moulded to the tightest buttocks and strongest-looking thighs Kitty had ever seen, did little to reduce her soaring blood-pressure. She, who never ogled men the way she'd seen some women do, was now having to exert every bit of will-power not to ogle him.

He stood between her and the sun, still waiting for an answer, it appeared.

'I don't want to expose myself to this sun,' she said gruffly. 'I've got such fair skin, I'll only burn.'

'I guess you will.' His eyes lightly roved from her pale jade T-shirt to her darker jade shorts. 'Oh, well, if I can't persuade you... here goes.'

He ran down to the water, splashing in up to his thighs before diving expertly into a wave, looking, she thought crossly, like the archetypal beach-bum.

She set out the picnic while he swam, and when she saw him dripping and half-naked, as he emerged from the water, little beads of sweat broke out on her forehead and she made a great show of dusting the big, ripe tomatoes with a napkin.

Her own appetite had, perhaps unsurprisingly, given the distraction sitting opposite her, deserted her. She half-heartedly chewed at some salad and bit into some bread, though she drank two glasses of the chilled white wine she'd brought. Darius showed no such restraint, tearing great hunks off the French stick, and devouring them with a disgustingly healthy appetite.

He took a swallow from his glass of wine, then turned on to his elbow, watching her.

'Stop fretting, Kitty,' he said abruptly. 'I'm not about to pounce on you.'

She turned her blue eyes upwards, stunned by the feeling of disappointment which rocketed through her. 'You're not?'

'Only if you want me to,' he murmured.

'I don't,' she said automatically, lowering her lashes in case he was able to read the lie in her eyes.

'Well, then, I don't particularly want to sail immediately after we've eaten—which leaves us with

half an hour or so to kill before we go back. What
else do you suggest we do?'

Put like that, by him, it was a loaded question.
'We could always chat,' she said unoriginally.

The stormy eyes glittered as a smile played around
the corner of his mouth. 'So we could,' he mused.
'What shall we talk about?'

'Always a conversation-killer,' she joked weakly.
'You think of something.'

'Why don't we play the truth game, Kitty?'

Her mouth fell open. She honestly thought that
her heart had frozen for an instant. 'Truth game?'
she whispered. 'What's that?'

'Surely you know? No? Never played it at
parties?' He paused. 'I can ask you any question I
like and you must answer it truthfully. You, in turn,
are free to ask me anything *you* like.'

She forced a laugh. 'Too embarrassing, surely?'

'We'll rely on our innate good taste,' he murmured. 'I'll begin.'

Kitty held her breath.

'What happens when your year with me is up?
Where do you go then?'

Her conscience had expected something far more
probing. The sooty lashes concealed his eyes, but
for a few moments he seemed so genuinely
interested that Kitty experienced an unwelcome
pang of guilt. But why should *she* feel guilty? After
all, he was the one who had taken the wretched
script.

She realised that she hadn't thought beyond this
job, and was now forced to improvise. 'I'd like to
see something else of Australia—the east coast.

Sydney harbour. Then maybe Tasmania, Fiji—maybe even New Zealand. It all depends on how long my money lasts.'

'And afterwards?' he prompted. 'When you've satisfied your wanderlust.'

'Home, probably. Back to England.'

'And what's in England? Do you have family?'

'My mother.'

'But no father?'

Something in the way he looked at her held her. Something about the searching glance from the silvery eyes made her want to expand. 'No, no father.' She swallowed as he continued to fix her with that steadfast gaze, wondering how she had ever allowed herself to be manoeuvred into a situation where she was confiding in him—worse still, *wanting* to confide in him. 'He died a couple of years ago—but he didn't live with us.'

'Why not?' Something about his watchfulness made her elaborate even further. Was that a skill he'd learnt as a film director—getting people to open up? Stripping away the layers of conditioned response so that the raw emotions lay exposed?

'He ran off with my mother's best friend,' she went on, as if compelled to. 'It hurt my mother much more because she is everything that a woman should be—incredibly beautiful—and Maggie—that's my stepmother—she was small, dumpy, fairly ordinary, really. But she filled my father's life with babies—and warmth—and love.' Which she supposed said more about her own mother than anything.

'And what about you, Kitty? Is that what you plan to do? Fill someone's house with babies, and warmth, and love?'

Colour seemed to invade every exposed bit of her flesh as she clamped down on the alarming vision of just whose babies she found herself wanting with a yearning which bordered on pain.

'Not in the foreseeable future,' she said quickly.

'So there's no hopeful boyfriend back in England?'

'Not——' And then, afraid that she would start pouring her heart out over Hugo, she changed the subject.

'It's my turn to ask something now, surely?' she asked lightly.

He rolled on to his side to lie on an elbow as he regarded her. 'Ask away.'

She wanted, she realised, to know whether anyone had ever got through to him, whether he had ever cared about anyone enough to fall in love with her, but she couldn't ask him that. She shouldn't ask him anything—she'd be leaving him soon—but today was a fantasy day where the future did not exist. 'What about your family?'

'Oh, my family,' he said slowly. 'I could provide a psychiatrist with a dream case-history.' He picked the glass up from the silvery white sand and swallowed some more wine. 'My mother was Welsh, my father Irish—we came over to the land of opportunity on a ten-pound package.'

'And was it—the land of opportunity?'

He gave a humourless smile. 'It sure was. Only trouble was that my father was the most work-shy

man ever put on this earth. He never managed to
keep a job longer than a week.'

She suddenly felt another unwelcome pang of
guilt as she saw the small boy in the face of the
man. 'Go on,' she said quietly, expecting him to
clam up, but to her surprise he didn't. Perhaps,
today, the need to confide was catching.

'I told you that my mother worked hard. She did
all those kind of jobs which mothers with useless
husbands have to do—she cleaned offices, houses,
pubs. But she hated leaving us—me and my sister.'

'Your sister?' asked Kitty in surprise.

He nodded. 'She's four years older. Married and
lives in the States now. I'm an uncle four times
over!'

And Kitty's lips softened automatically as she
heard the ring of pride in his voice. 'You were
saying?' she prompted gently. 'About your
mother?'

He gave a shrug which did nothing to disguise
the rigidity of his broad shoulders. 'She was brilliant with kids and she wanted to child-mind—that
would have kept her at home with us—but the
authorities always refused to give permission. With
barely any income from my father, our house was
too small and basic to provide space for more
children. So she worked herself into the ground.'
There was a long pause. 'She died when I was
fifteen. She never saw me achieve anything. She
never knew how much I owed to her.'

Kitty forgot about everything, for the pain on his
face eclipsed everything; she forgot all her doubts,
fears, regrets and suspicions. Tentatively, she

reached out and put her hand over his, squeezing it in a gesture of comfort such as a nurse would give to a sick patient, and he looked up, his grey eyes clearing into an expression of surprise, almost, thought Kitty, as if he was not used to women touching him in any way which wasn't sexual.

'I'm sure she knew,' Kitty said softly. 'Maybe she knows, even now.' She said it with a kind of calm certainty which came from somewhere deep within her.

His eyes met hers, and this time, very slowly, travelled over her face, inch by inch, as though he had awoken from a dream—taking in the blue fire of her eyes, the red froth of her curls which had escaped from her plait and were blowing gently in the breeze. The moment was stage-set for a kiss, so that when he moved forward it came as no surprise. In fact this too had an almost dream-like quality as he gathered her into his arms and bent his head to stare down at her, his face a series of shifting planes, dark and unreadable, his silver eyes alive with a piercing light.

But he didn't kiss her; for seconds he simply stared, as though, if he stared long enough, he would be able to see into her soul.

'Which is the real Kitty?' he whispered. 'Is she soft and caring and malleable? Is that who you really are?'

Her heart thudded with both danger and desire. 'Who else could I be?' she asked lightly.

He ignored her question. 'What do you want from me?' he demanded.

She dared not admit the answer even to herself. 'What do you want from me?' she parried shakily.

He smiled then—slow, sure, confident and controlled. 'I want *this*,' he murmured as he slowly bent his head towards her. 'And so do you.'

Colour flooded up to fan her cheekbones, and lethargy invaded her limbs as his words of desire seduced her. Too late she tried to reason with herself. She wasn't here to be seduced by this man with the decadent past. She was on a mission for Caro.

But as she stared up at him she realised something fundamentally more important—just what exactly had been bothering her ever since she'd known him. *She didn't believe he'd done it.*

Darius was many things: he could be quick-tempered and sarcastic—a perfectionist who expected nothing less from the people who worked for him. He was also undeniably sexy—and women were turned on by him in droves. But he was not a manipulator—of that she was certain. And he was not a thief. He was a man who had risen to the top in spite of the worst kind of start, who inspired long-standing affection in people like Simon.

And somewhere along the way she had fallen in love with him... And, whatever his feelings for her, she wanted him. For the first time in her life she wanted to listen to the demands of her heart. What if she said no to him, then spent the rest of her life regretting that decision?

Wide-eyed she stared up at him and, as he began to kiss her, she realised that the wait was over.

His mouth brushed hers, his tongue moving to trace the outline of her lips in a butterfly movement of sensual perfection. Her eyelids fluttered to a close as his mouth continued its leisurely exploration, and it was the slowest, most delectable feast imaginable.

He pulled her closer, into the hard warmth of his chest, and she could feel his heart hammering against the soft pliancy of her breast.

The kiss went on and on and it seemed to take forever before he touched her more intimately, and she gave a little cry when one hand slipped underneath her T-shirt to cup her aching breast, but his touch was no intrusion—no intrusion at all. It seemed the most natural thing in the world, and Kitty knew such an overwhelming need that she threw her arms tightly around his neck and kissed him back with an ardent fervour, pressing herself close to him in unconscious invitation, and it was at that moment that he stopped kissing her.

Dizzily she opened her eyes, feeling the melting longing between her thighs, knowing that he could do anything he liked with her, and she wouldn't want to resist, when he suddenly moved away, holding her trembling body at arm's length.

He shook his head. 'No,' he said, his voice harsh, an indefinable note in it.

'No?' she echoed dimly.

'So no doubts today, then, Kitty?' he said, a touch of barely restrained savagery clipping each word. 'I could take you now, right here, on the sand—and you'd let me, wouldn't you?'

'I . . .' But she blushed, unable to deny the truth, wondering what had caused his anger, what had caused him to stop kissing her so suddenly. She stared at him in confusion, and then at last the set, angry look disappeared and he gave a small smile.

'But I don't want it that way,' he said silkily. 'Not here. Not the first time—like this—where we could be disturbed. I want to make the slowest love to you in the world, Kitty. Once I start, I don't want to stop. I want to take you home. To my bed.'

Her heart swelled with love as she realised that he was not angry, he was merely being protective. She rose to her feet, brushing the fine sand from her thighs, saw his eyes hungrily follow the movement, which had unwittingly been provocative, and she smiled, experiencing for the first time in her life the heady power of her own sexuality. She held out her hand to him, the desire she saw written on his face making her suddenly, supremely confident. 'Then let's go.'

His eyes were iron-hard as he rose to join her, catching her by the shoulders and staring down into her face. 'I don't want you to let me make love to you because we got carried away on a beach one hot and sultry day. I want you to think very carefully about what it is you want.' And then he said something totally unexpected, his face suddenly unsmiling once more, his eyes glittering. 'I'm giving you time to change your mind, Kitty.' There was an abstruse note to his voice which puzzled her. She half imagined that she heard the glimmer of a warning, but then he smiled once more, a bright, blinding and totally irresistible smile.

Her heart sang. This had to be the craziest thing she had ever done in her life, but somehow she didn't care. She felt dizzy with excited longing. 'I'm not going to change my mind,' she murmured.

He didn't duplicate his brilliant smile; instead his eyes narrowed, as if he was surprised by the cool certainty of her actions. But then, this would inevitably mean more to her than it would to him, and she mustn't forget that. She bent to pick up the empty wine bottle, but he suddenly scooped her back up against his chest, giving a small moan.

'How do you expect me to steer the boat back,' he demanded urgently, 'when you've got me so worked up?'

She could feel his erection pressing against her buttocks, and, untutored though she was, nevertheless some instinct couldn't prevent her from gently urging herself further against him, moving her bottom in an enticing little circle, until he pushed her away, as if scalded.

'For God's sake, Kitty,' he said harshly, 'what are you trying to do to me?' He turned her round and kissed her again, and the kiss was less controlled this time, and then, releasing her, he knelt down, his bare knees embedded in the sand as he began hurling the refuse from the picnic into the cool-box.

He sat back on his heels, his mouth curved in a wry, self-deprecating smile. 'Let's go,' he said, 'before you tempt me into making love to you, despite all my protestations. It's a pity that in public places, it remains illegal . . .'

CHAPTER TEN

KITTY couldn't quite decide whether the journey back was pleasure or pain. It was certainly too long!

The waiting, the anticipation, set her senses singing, her blood pumping around her body as it had never done before. She'd made a decision and she was going to stick to it. They were going home, like adults, to make love. Theirs hadn't been just a hasty coupling on the sand—Darius was taking her home, to make love to her properly, in comfort and in privacy, taking all the time in the world.

They spoke very little. Now that she had made her decision, she felt strangely shy, glad enough to watch Darius as he controlled the yacht, feasting her eyes on him while he worked.

The urge to smother every inch of his body with kisses was overpowering, but she had enough sense not to. Men liked independent females—not slavish devotion!

Am I really in love with him? she wondered as she stared at his hard, beautiful profile. I don't know him very well. Up until about an hour ago, I believed him guilty of theft—so how, now, can I suddenly believe myself to be in love with him?

Because love was unpredictable, not something which could be measured out like an equation. You couldn't decide that after, say, twenty hours in a man's company you would then know him well enough to decide whether or not you were in love with him. Sometimes it just hit you—like a summer squall.

But by the time they had driven back to the house, second thoughts had begun to assail her. This was *her* after all. A fairly ordinary working cook—hardly in the same class as the lauded film-maker.

The front door had closed behind them, and she turned to face him, trembling again, but this time with sheer regret at her hot-headedness. 'Darius...' Her voice tailed off. 'Maybe you were right. Maybe I've changed my mind. Perhaps this isn't such a good idea after all.'

His face revealed nothing. He was not a bully like Hugo, she thought as she stared up at him. He wouldn't dream of trying to force her. It was her decision and he would take it or leave it—and it was then that she knew without a doubt that she didn't want him to leave it!

'Don't you want to make love?' he asked softly, his grey eyes searching.

Oh, when he said it like that! When he looked at her like that! 'I...I... Yes, I do,' she said honestly.

'Well, then.' He smiled as he took her by the hand. 'Come here.'

She supposed she had been expecting him to lead her directly to his bedroom, and was half pleased, half disappointed when he took her straight into the sitting-room.

He sat her down on one of the big chintz sofas, and turned to the cabinet to pick up a bottle of wine and open it. 'You look,' he remarked, 'petrified. As if you've never done this kind of thing before.'

She took a huge mouthful of the wine he handed her, thankfully feeling it filling her with warmth. This was her chance. The time to tell him that deep down she suspected she might be frigid, and that she was a virgin to boot.

She couldn't.

She took another huge swallow of wine, then the glass was gently taken from her hand and placed on the small table by the sofa. She noticed that he'd drunk nothing himself.

'You don't need any more of that,' he said, and sat down beside her, staring at her hair in its severe plait. 'Take your hair down,' he said suddenly. 'Take it down—for me.'

She lifted her hands to her head, but her fingers were trembling too much. 'I can't,' she whispered. 'See.'

He didn't say a word, just slowly began to unpick the thick braid, until her curls lay free and unfettered, falling over her shoulders in a fiery tangle.

'Now, do you know what I'm going to do to you?' he whispered, his hands massaging her spine until every bit of tension had died away.

'No,' she said, her voice shaking with excitement.

'First of all I'm going to kiss you. Like this.'

She sighed as his mouth found hers, her lips parting immediately, and his tongue explored the hot, moist interior with dizzying effect. She didn't know how long he kissed her for, only that she found herself lying back on the sofa, with him beside her, one hard thigh thrust between hers.

'Then,' he tore his mouth away to whisper gently against her neck, 'I'm going to touch your breasts. Like this...'

She gave a little moan of disbelief as his fingers reached the swollen mounds of her breasts. His hand snaked round her back and he unclasped her bra in a single movement.

'It's strapless,' he murmured approvingly as he pulled it off and dropped it over the side of the sofa, before dipping his head and taking a taut and erect nipple into his mouth.

'Oh... *oh*,' she gasped, her hands flailing wildly at her sides as his tongue licked her there with voluptuous and tantalising skill.

'And then...' He spoke against the nipple, and she felt the vibrations of his speech tingling up through her chest. 'Then I'm going to touch you *here*...' His mouth carried on suckling while his fingertips scorched an erotic path up to the top of her thighs, moving aside the suddenly intrusive barrier of silky panties to skate lightly and tantalisingly over and over the acutely aroused skin, before at last delving into her hot and private haven.

She gave a shuddering, almost helpless sigh, and reached her hand down tentatively to brush her fingers against his hardness, which strained so much against the zip of his denim shorts that she was surprised it hadn't snapped. Her eyelids flew open as her hand covered his arousal, and for the first time she wondered fleetingly if it would hurt, as all the books said it would.

'That's good,' he said unsteadily. '*Very* good.' And then his voice changed to a harsh note which sounded almost like a desperate plea. 'Kitty—we'd better get to the bedroom. And quickly. Because if we don't . . .'

He hadn't moved his hand, and she felt the moist hotness of herself throbbing in expectation as she enfolded his finger. She wanted him. *Now*.

'I don't think I can move,' she sighed truthfully.

'And I don't think that I'm in any fit state to carry you,' he husked ruefully.

He moved away from her, pulled off her shorts and her panties then her T-shirt, so that she was naked, and she shut her eyes, suddenly shy. There was silence for a moment, which caused her to open her eyes, and when she did it was to see him staring at her body, his eyes as dark as the night.

She watched as he began to remove his own clothes, and the sight of his masculine nakedness, bronzed apart from a white strip where he'd obviously worn swimming-trunks, filled her with a sudden sense of longing, so acute that she reached her arms up to him, pulling him down on top of her, her mouth as urgent as his as they rained kiss upon kiss on each other's lips.

As she clung to him, she forgot everything except the sensation of his skin touching hers, of his closeness, of his hands and his mouth inflicting erotic torture, until she was stirring beneath him, her hips thrusting impatiently towards his hardness.

She heard him give a low laugh.

'Now this,' he said, on a breaking note of desire, '*this* is what I want to do to you more than anything else...'

He entered her with slow, exquisite, breath-taking control, and she gave nothing more than the merest shudder as he broke through the barrier and possessed her, because there was only the most fleeting hint of pain—for, though his arousal was devastating, she was so pliant, so ready for him, that it was as if her body had been waiting all its life for this one moment.

But that one moment was just the beginning.

As he began to move, with swift, sure movements, she realised that the intense feeling deep at the very core of her was growing all the time. She felt her cheeks on fire as he thrust into her, sometimes teasing her with provocative withdrawal until she could bear it no more, and she thought that she must have uttered an incoherent plea, or perhaps he could just see how close she was to the edge, because he began to move within her with a hard wildness which was shockingly thrilling until, at last, something very close to magic caught her up in its spell.

'Oh! *No*!' she cried out in shocked disbelief as wave upon wave of unbelievable pleasure began to engulf her, sending her soaring.

'Oh, *yes*,' he urged. '*Yes*!'

She heard him give a low moan as he drove into her deeply one last time, and felt him give one great shudder, and, her own orgasm still fading, she dimly wrapped her arms tightly about him, cradling him against her sweat-slicked breasts as he sank down on top of her.

Languorously she kissed his bare shoulder, loving the feeling of being bonded with him, loving the feeling of closeness. She wanted to hear—what? Words of love?

No, she wasn't naïve enough to expect that. But something, surely? As their breathing stilled, she waited, but still he said nothing and, although disappointed, she was too blissfully contented to allow her insecurity to spoil the magic of the moment...

She must have drifted off, because when her eyelids fluttered open it was to find him awake too, staring up at the ceiling, a thoughtful look on his face, and she wondered what he was thinking about. What did men usually think about at times like this? Was she supposed to get up, or stay? Would it be all right for her to begin to explore *his* body now, as she longed to? Or should she wait for him to make the first move? He must have sensed that she too was awake for he turned to her, still unsmiling, his face an impassive mask that was impossible to read.

'Let's go to bed,' he said.

'I'll be back soon.' He pulled a white cotton T-shirt over his head.

How soon? she wondered, but she didn't say it. 'OK.' She gave it, she thought, just the right degree of nonchalance, when if the truth were known she would have happily chained herself to his leg and begged him to take her with him!

She leaned back against the bank of disarrayed pillows and surveyed him, his hair still damp from his early-morning shower. She felt as if she couldn't bear him to be away from her for more than a minute. In possessing her physically, he had also irretrievably bound her to him spiritually. She wondered whether he felt bound to her in any way whatsoever.

He sat down on the edge of the bed, his hand drifting down the side of her face to brush over her bare breast. Boldly she captured it there, but, smiling, he moved it away. 'Not now,' he said, shaking his head. 'I have a plane to catch, remember?'

'I'll see you tomorrow.' She pushed a heavy strand of mussed hair off her face, her heart pattering as she saw the flash of desire in his eyes.

He shook his head. 'Don't you believe it. I'll try and get back tonight. Late. Simon will be in around ten to collect the mail and deal with anything that's urgent. Apart from that you'll have the house to yourself. I've phoned Janet and told her not to bother coming in.' He leaned over her, picking up a lock of the red hair which lay fanned across the pillow. 'Beautiful girl,' he whispered as he planted a kiss on top of her head. 'Goodbye.'

She crossed her fingers as he said it. It seemed an unlucky word, as if saying it might make it come true.

She put on her crumpled clothes, then went straight into her own annexe, showered, washed her hair and dressed in clean shorts and T-shirt.

Sooner or later she was going to have to tell Caro what had happened—that she hadn't managed to retrieve the script at all. That instead she had fallen in love with Darius and had become his lover. And that there must have been some mix-up, some kind of misunderstanding, because she simply couldn't believe that he'd done what Caro had accused him of.

She went to the kitchen to make herself some coffee. It just didn't make sense, she thought. If only she could actually *prove* that her instincts were right.

The thought troubled her all morning, all through having coffee with Simon, who, she thought, looked at her oddly once or twice, which made her wonder whether he could see the physical effects of Darius's night-long lovemaking written all over her face.

She couldn't eat lunch and she fretted all afternoon, until, eventually, she did what she had been wanting to do all day and walked slowly through the big house and into Darius's study.

It was a beautiful room, full of exquisitely chosen antique furniture. On the one deep blue wall which wasn't lined with books hung some contemporary oil-paintings, which should have clashed and been at odds with the furnishings but somehow created a strikingly successful blend.

She looked at the books which lined the shelves from floor to ceiling—books on just about every subject in the world. She thought about how hard he must have worked to overcome the social disadvantages of his background...

Her eyes swept downwards to the computer, which *did* look incongruously modern on the polished mahogany of the huge desk. There was a sheaf of papers fanned out, his spiky black writing distinctive. Idly, her eyes scanned the title-page and saw *To Do or Die*, and a great rush of dizziness swept over her.

It was part of the film-script he was working on!

He was paranoid about people stealing his ideas—even Simon had said that. And he kept all his work safely locked away.

Kitty knew that here she had the perfect opportunity. She could simply put the script away, and...

And?

She picked up the telephone and dialled Simon's home number, her hand trembling.

'Simon,' she said, without preamble. 'I happened to be walking past Darius's study——' the lie slipped from her lips with terrifying ease '—when I found part of the script of the film he's writing lying on his desk.'

'Strewth!' said Simon. 'Pretty careless of him.'

'Yes. The thing is that I know he's hot on security and I wondered—shall I just put it in the safe?'

'No worries—I can do that.'

'I just thought it would save you making the journey over...'

Simon laughed. 'What a thoughtful girl you are, Kitty. That's fine. Go ahead.'

She drew in a deep breath. 'The trouble is that I don't have the combination of his safe.'

There was a long silence; for a minute she thought that the line had been disconnected. 'Hello—Simon?'

His voice came back on. 'Sorry, Kitty—I thought I heard someone at the door. What was that you wanted? The combination of his safe?'

She managed to keep the shake out of her voice. 'That's right.'

'Have you got a pen?'

'Yes.'

'OK—it's four-seven-one-three-seven-eight-eight. Got that?'

'Four-seven-one-three-seven-eight-eight,' she repeated. 'Yes. Thank you, Simon.

She didn't move from the chair for a moment or two. She wanted to know and yet she didn't want to know. I don't care, she thought stubbornly. 'I *have* to know. And who would ever know she'd even looked?

Her heart was thudding like a piston as she went over to the wall and pulled the picture back to reveal the safe. It was an old-fashioned kind, with a heavy brass numbered dial. With an effort, she began to turn the numbers out. Four-seven-one-three-seven-eight-eight.

Just as in the films, the door gave with a little click. Heavily it swung open, revealing a whole stack of small files, and Kitty drew in a deep breath as she put her hand inside.

First of all she put the script in one corner, then, with trembling fingers, she began to flick through the neatly labelled files.

'Hello, Kitty,' came a deep, drawling voice from behind her. 'Looking for something?'

CHAPTER ELEVEN

KITTY whirled round, her heart crashing against her ribs, to find Darius standing there, his face as dark as the devil's.

She opened her mouth to speak, but found herself temporarily mute.

'I said,' he reiterated menacingly, 'are you looking for something?'

'I—thought you'd flown up to Tom Price,' she croaked.

'Let's just say I changed my mind,' he answered cuttingly. 'And please don't change the subject. I asked you a question.' His eyes flicked over her frightened face with distaste. 'Can't quite decide the best way to answer? Then I'll help you out, shall I, Kitty? Shall I try and guess how your tortured little thought-processes actually work? Why don't you sit down? This could take some time.' He gestured to the black leather chair she stood beside.

'I—don't want to sit down,' she croaked again through dry lips. But her knees chose that very moment to give way, and she flopped down into the chair.

'I'm really not quite sure whether to call the police,' he said, almost conversationally, as though he were deciding on a choice of shirt-colour.

The vision of him, towering and darkly menacing, swam before her eyes. 'You—wouldn't...?'

'Wouldn't I?' The grey eyes were like cold metal on a winter morning. 'Why not? I surprised you in the act of theft, didn't I?' he asked deliberately. 'Who set you up? Was it the papers—looking for a juicy tit-bit? Or are you out to steal my work—with your eye on the main chance? My God, I knew that I should have listened to my head—I knew all along that you weren't to be trusted.'

She felt sick. He *had* suspected her all along. 'You knew?' she whispered.

'Yes, I knew,' he agreed, and must have seen her look of horror. 'Oh, not for certain until just now—I give you that. I couldn't put my finger on it when you first arrived, but my job is to observe human behaviour, and your behaviour was distinctly odd.' He stared at her with insolent frankness. 'You were, you see, unlike any woman I'd ever met. Or so I thought. For a start, you were fighting the attraction you felt towards me—and women rarely do that,' he concluded arrogantly. He leaned forward and poured himself a small snifter of brandy from the tray of bottles on the desk, drinking it off in a single draught before putting the empty glass down on the desk and staring at her once more.

'And yet, at times, you seemed almost frightened of me. It was intriguing, and I am rarely intrigued by a woman.' He poured himself another brandy, and drank that too. 'And then you seemed to relax and, I must admit, I allowed myself to be taken in by your *supposed* soft-heartedness, the way you

made me want to keep the cat, your kindness with
the child next door. God, you were convincing. And
of course I wanted you, *very* much, and I'm afraid
that I let desire blind me.' He gave her a cold, empty
smile which indicated with frightening clarity that
he was no longer blinded by any such need. He
folded his arms across his chest as he continued,
so that he looked as burly and as menacing as a
nightclub bouncer. 'And so I quashed the little an-
noying suspicions I had about you—refused to let
them rear their ugly heads.

'But the day you borrowed the car you alerted
all those dormant suspicions, and you were right,
I *did* follow you to the employment agency. Your
guilt at being discovered convinced me that my suspicions were not without foundation. I remembered how, when you arrived, I'd found you
skulking around my bedroom after tripping into my
study. I remembered how jumpy you were, and how
fearful at times. I asked myself, Could it be that
you were not the sweet innocent you professed to
be? That you were here with some express purpose
in mind? That you were looking for something?'

She buried her head in her hands. 'But why didn't
you ask me?' she cried, raising her eyes to his, remembering the closeness she had thought they'd
shared. The swim. The talks over tea. 'Why didn't
you confront me with your suspicions?'

His mouth became a cold, implacable line, and
a look of pure disgust radiated from his eyes. 'Oh,
come *on*, Kitty,' he said coldly. 'And have you lie
to me? Your type always do.'

'Your type'. Kitty shivered in revulsion.

'Besides,' he continued relentlessly, 'I was interested to know just how far you'd go to get whatever information you were after. I must say that I was surprised to find out that you'd pay the ultimate price to get what you wanted.'

Bile rose in her throat. 'You mean—that...you...'

'No, sweetheart, *you*,' he corrected her coldly. 'You thought that there was one way you could win my trust, and, by God, you took it! You were prepared to sleep with me in order to break into my safe——'

He actually believed that! She gripped the desk, her knuckles white, a white rage enveloping her. 'Well, what about you? You're no better! You tricked me! You slept with me knowing that you were going to denounce me! That's the most cold-hearted thing I could ever imagine!'

'Hardly cold-hearted,' he contradicted her insolently. 'Quite the opposite, in fact.'

'If you knew, then why the hell didn't you confront me before?' she sobbed. Instead of humiliating me, using me like some worthless little tart, she added silently.

He gave a small laugh. 'Oh, please, Kitty. Let's not be naïve. I told you, I wanted you, and if you were prepared to go all the way for what you wanted...well...I'm only human.' He shrugged expressively.

'You bastard!' she shouted. 'You low-down, stinking *bastard*!' She stared at him. 'That's why Simon gave me the combination so readily, isn't it? The film-script. You left it on your desk deliber-

ately, knowing that with it I had a perfectly legit-
imate excuse to open the safe.'

'Let's just call it a carrot which I dangled before
you. Oh, I wanted to believe that you wouldn't take
it, but...' He shrugged. 'Instead of going to the
airport, I went round to Simon's. I was there when
you phoned. He told me how insistent you were
that you should have the combination. I came
straight back here to catch you in the act, as they
say. Tell me, Kitty, what exactly was it that you
wanted so badly?'

Her mouth tightened with disgust. 'As if you
didn't know!' she yelled. 'You heartless, cheating
thief! How you have the *audacity* to stand there
with that sanctimonious look all over your face,
lecturing me about *my* morals I just don't know!

'At least I'm true to myself!' she raged. 'I don't
go building up an empire on the backs of other
people's talent! I don't go about robbing old ladies
and plagiarising their work!

'You disgust me, Darius Speed—almost as much
as I disgust myself! To think that I was almost taken
in by you. To think that I almost believed there'd
been some mix-up, that Caro——'

'Caro?' he queried, his dark eyebrows arched.

'Yes, Caro! Caro Peters! Of Caro's Kitchen
Cookies! Don't try and play the innocent with me!
God,' she said, 'you weren't the only one who was
taken in. I must have been lulled into a state of
temporary insanity. For a while back there I
actually thought that you were a fundamentally
decent man—that you couldn't possibly have stolen
Caro's film-script!'

'Oh, yeah?' he mocked. 'Interesting little fairy-tale, Kitty—but it still doesn't explain what you were doing with your hands in my safe. Looking for some flour for your cookies, maybe?'

'*Oh*!' In a moment of blind anger, she leaned forward, poured some brandy into the same snifter he had used, and flung it all over his face. 'I *hate* you!' she yelled, and glared at him across the desk, before realising in horror just what she'd done, expecting him to retaliate in some way; but he didn't move a muscle.

Even the brandy dripping brown tears all over his white T-shirt didn't seem to make him look a fool, she thought angrily.

His mouth twisted into a sardonic line. 'Personally I think you're wasting your talents as a cook, Kitty. Because for a moment back there when you were making love you acted like you really meant it, rather than it being a means to an end. You know, you could make a very fine actress,' he mused.

'Go to hell!' She rose from the chair on feet which were surprisingly steady.

'And of course——' and here the grey eyes pointedly scanned her heaving breasts '—there's another profession you'd *really* excel at—but I wouldn't advise that. It has a limited life-span and is fraught with dangers.'

'Go to hell!' she yelled again as she stormed out of the room, thinking how difficult it was to be creative with insults when you were this angry.

Kitty ran straight from the study, out into the garden and then into her annexe, where she im-

mediately took her suitcases down and began
packing—hurling clothes in indiscriminately, not
caring whether they were ruined, so keen was she
to put miles between herself and Darius.

She cursed silently as garments were fired in like
missiles, maintaining the momentum of her anger,
because at least anger was something strong, something which would prevent her from crumbling,
from going under and giving way to tears which she
was sure she could never stem once they had started.

Only once did her lip quiver and that was when
she thought of Mersey. Would Darius have the de-
cency to continue letting the cat live in his house?

She slammed the cases closed. He might have
treated her like—like... She bit her lip. Even if
Darius decided that *she* would have to go, she
doubted whether even he would kick a three-legged
cat out on to the street.

She was struggling up the path and back into the
house when she almost bumped into Darius. He
didn't look surprised to see her suitcases.

'You're going?' he said abruptly.

She held her chin up. 'No—I'm carrying these
around for the sake of my health!'

He didn't react. 'Where will you go?'

'That's none of your business!'

'I'd better drive you.'

'No, thanks.'

'Kitty——'

'I'd sooner walk all the way in bare feet over *nails*
than get into your car. Now, if you'll kindly let me
pass.'

'Then I'll call a taxi.'

She whirled round. When would he start getting the message? 'I said, No, *thanks*!'

'There's an envelope on the hall table. It contains your salary.'

In a film she would have flung the envelope back in his face or, better still, ripped the money into tiny shreds and let them flutter to the ground in front of him like confetti. But the reality was entirely different. She was not in a film. She was alone, in a city miles away from home, and she needed the money. True, tomorrow she could cable home for some—but her pride balked at that, especially since her mother had been so against her coming here in the first place. And therefore she needed every cent towards her air-ticket home.

Somehow, she managed to get herself and her suitcases out on to the street and walked until she found a call-box and rang for a cab, but she stared at the driver blankly when he said, 'Where to?'

'I don't know,' she said, suddenly frightened, and burst into tears. And perhaps the cab-driver was afraid that she was in no fit state to be alone, for she found herself being taken to a bed-and-breakfast place without having asked, where he spoke in hurried undertones to a motherly-looking creature who took one look at her before bundling her into a basic but comfortable and clean room.

The woman put a cup of strong, steaming tea down in front of Kitty, and left her alone to cry.

CHAPTER TWELVE

KITTY'S first impulse was, naturally, to run away. If not back to England, then maybe to the east coast—to Sydney. Or to the Gold Coast, or perhaps to Queensland.

But she thought about all the alternatives which faced her, and one by one she rejected them.

For a start, she was not going crawling back to England. She could just imagine what her mother would say. She had been advised against making such an epic journey on her own, and if she went back—having suffered another, but much worse, broken heart—that would be more or less what her mother had expected.

And running to a different part of Australia would be more of the same. Basically, it would be telling Darius that she couldn't cope, even—God forbid—that she was heart-broken. And she wasn't, was she? Not heart-broken.

Not at all. The tears that soaked her pillows at night were an indication of her sense of dismay that she had been betrayed so readily by the man she had believed herself to be in love with. How *could* he have made love to her just before setting her up? Obviously everything that Caro had told her about him had been true. It had been she who had stupidly wanted to believe otherwise.

Well, that, as her mother always said, was men for you. And Kitty, for one, was going to emerge from this whole sorry incident with her pride intact.

Didn't they say that the worst of life's experiences proved spiritually rewarding, making you mentally much stronger? Well, just you wait, Darius Speed, she thought with determination. I'm going to end up with a mind the size of a colossus!

Her resolve wavered a bit, especially first thing in the morning and last thing at night, but by and large she felt quite proud of herself.

Firstly, she had to find herself a job, but she couldn't bring herself to face Caro. She wasn't up to the post-mortem into how she'd failed. Quite frankly, she couldn't face seeing anyone who knew her even vaguely, for fear that her carefully maintained front would crumble and they would see the terrible desolation in her eyes.

She went for the kind of job which she wished to high heaven she'd done before. It was all the things that she had told Darius she didn't want.

She trailed around every good restaurant, clutching all her qualifications, and, amazingly, became commis-chef in a prestigious restaurant on the waterfront, owned by a man named Brent Salisbury whom she met at her interview—a tall, imposing blond Australian who was married to an equally blonde, imposing wife. Brent now had a string of restaurants interstate, but rarely spent any of his evenings in them, since his wife had recently presented him with a blond, imposing and extremely noisy baby.

His head chef was Paolo—a flamboyant, temperamental genius, half-Irish and half-Italian. Paolo, still in his mid-twenties, was what was known as a celebrity chef, because, as well as being known for his culinary talents, he was always being featured in the gossip-columns with a variety of stunning women. That Kitty, sick at heart over Darius, failed to respond to his abundant charm seemed to amuse him.

'You see?' he would remark to the kitchen staff at large in his flamboyant way. 'She is the quintessential English girl. So cool. So icy. So untouchable.'

And Kitty would slice up a peeled cucumber in record time, smiling with gritted teeth but saying nothing.

She had been there less than a week when there was a commotion in the kitchen.

Firstly, the head waiter was dispatched from the restaurant to ask the chef to join a customer for a glass of champagne. This seemed to happen fairly regularly, from what Kitty had seen.

'Is a woman?' asked Paolo.

'A man,' answered the waiter. 'Not the usual type.'

Paolo disappeared, returning minutes later with a broad smile fixed to his face. He waggled his finger at Kitty. 'Aha! Now I know why it is that you do not respond to me in any way that a woman should.'

Kitty glanced up, every single strand of her ginger hair hidden by the all-enveloping chef's hat. 'What?'

'Because now I see that your heart belongs to another.'

'What *are* you talking about?'

Paolo was in full flow, playing up his Italian side like mad. 'This man—he is not interested in my food—a whole plateful he leave untouched. He is more interested in my staff, and in particular a young woman member of my staff. In you, Kitty.'

She asked the totally unnecessary question. 'What did he look like?'

Paolo shrugged. 'He is tall. He is dark. He is handsome—some might say more handsome than me, but I do not think so. The lines of his face are too hard, too harsh.'

Kitty's heart had started beating very quickly. 'What did you say?' she whispered.

'I told him that, yes, you work here. Then he demand that he see you. He *demanded*! Of me! I told him that he could not——'

'Thank God,' breathed Kitty.

'That he did not deserve to see you if he is the person responsible for those dark shadows, that little pinched face——'

'Oh, Paolo—you *didn't*.'

'Sure I did,' he grinned. 'And, because I know that nothing turns a man on more than jealousy, I told him that I was taking you out this afternoon after we closed.'

Kitty nearly took the top of her thumb off, and laid the knife down with a shaking hand. 'You really shouldn't——'

But she never got a chance to complete the sentence, because at that moment there was a flurry at the swing doors which led into the kitchen, and there stood Darius, his face grimly set and determined, his eyes fixed on Kitty.

'Get *out* of my kitchen!' screamed Paolo.

Darius didn't move a muscle. 'Come on, Kitty,' he said. 'I need to talk to you.'

She gave him a look of sheer blue ice. 'Tough. I've nothing to say to you.' Memories of just how stupidly she had behaved over him sent her temper flaring. 'Get out, you conniving, scheming, hateful *bastard*!'

The tirade appeared to have gone right over his head. 'I'm not leaving here without you.'

His voice was like chocolate, she thought, rich, dark, smooth chocolate. And I'm not going to fall for it again. 'Then you'll have a long wait, Darius. As you can see, I'm working. I have a job to do, and I'm damned well going to do it.'

'Bravo!' interjected Paolo.

'Then I'll wait,' Darius said coolly, and, to Kitty's astonishment and outrage, he calmly walked over to the other side of the kitchen, perched on one of the high stools, took what looked like a film-script out of his pocket, and began working on it. The cheek of the man!

'You can't stay there!' Kitty blustered.

'Want to bet?' he asked softly, not even raising his dark head from the page.

'Paolo...' she beseeched softly, but to her dismay her boss was shrugging and rolling his eyes dramatically. 'When a man is that determined it is better that you see him. Of course——' he looked at her questioningly, a sparkle in his eyes as his fiery

Latin nature anticipated even more drama '—I
could always call the police?'

She should have said yes, but somehow she
couldn't, and she shook her head. Not, she thought
grimly as she picked up her knife, that the police
would do anything. He would exude that same kind
of cool assurance, and they would probably take
his side as Paolo had—like the horrible band of
conspiratorial males they were.

'Or you could go early?' Paolo suggested.

'No, thanks.' No way! Let him sit there while she
worked. He could stay there until three, when she
usually finished, and she hoped that he got a stiff
back for his trouble!

Unfortunately, trying to proceed as normal was
easier said than done. She tried to concentrate on
the job in hand, forcing herself to distinguish between the smells of the food, concentrating with
deliberate intensity on the textures she was helping
Paolo to create, when all the time there were different fragrances and textures which filled her mind.
She found herself remembering the silkiness of
Darius's hair, the smooth satin feel of his skin, and
the shockingly hard strength of the muscle beneath. Instead of lemon and cumin, her nostrils
were assailed with that particular scent of the man
who had briefly been her lover.

Every now and again she would steal a glance in
his direction, and once or twice their eyes met, and
when she saw the glimmer of some unholy
amusement in his she forced herself to glower back.

The end of the shift took forever to arrive. She
felt like Cinderella as she pulled off her uniform in

the cloakroom, washed her face and tied her hair back even more tightly than usual, like a schoolgirl's, deliberately adopting as unflattering a guise as possible, because the last thing she wanted was for him to look at her with desire. She didn't trust her own ability to resist him ...

She came out of the cloakroom and was hoisting her blue leather satchel over her shoulder when she felt him behind her. Not that he touched her—he didn't have to. She could hear the sound of his breathing without looking, her nostrils recognising that warm, masculine, soapy scent of him.

She turned on him furiously. 'How *dare* you come marching in here like that, as if you owned the place?'

'But I do,' he said coolly. 'Well, half of it, anyway.'

This completely took the wind out of her sails. '*What* did you say?'

He shrugged. 'I was at university with Brent Salisbury. When he started out he was short of cash—I knew how precarious the film industry could be and wanted something to fall back on if my first venture failed—so I invested in his first restaurant, and subsequent ones. I'm what you call a sleeping partner—except,' he concluded on a grim note, 'that I haven't been getting very much sleep lately. I've had the devil of a job finding you,' he accused. 'You shouldn't have rushed away like that.' He shook his head a little. 'Ironic, really, that I happened to ask Brent if he'd heard of you working at any other restaurant in the city, and discovered that he had employed you himself.'

She couldn't believe what she was hearing. She honestly couldn't believe it. Of all the insufferable, arrogant...! 'What did you think I would do, Darius?' she demanded. 'Stand and listen to all the dreadful things you said about me, and then hang around waiting for more?'

'I lost my temper,' he said slowly. 'I shouldn't have done that. I didn't want you to go.'

'Well, you did a very good imitation of wanting me to, then!' She shook her head tiredly. 'Oh, what's the point of raking it all up now?'

'There's a very good point,' he said, still in that same grim tone. 'Now let's go. I've got the car outside.'

She thought of herself, alone with him in a car, trapped... She shook her head. 'No, Darius. I'm not going anywhere with you, not in the car, or——'

'Kitty.' He spoke with the voice of a man at the very end of his patience. 'You have two choices. Either you get in the car like a good girl or I put you into it by force.' He heard her sharp intake of breath. 'And don't think that I wouldn't, either.'

She was furious with herself, but he wasn't to know that her sharp-breathed reaction had been one of dizzy, if reluctant, excitement. The thought of Darius, like some caveman, carrying her to his car... She stuck her nose in the air and climbed into the passenger seat of the Porsche, saying nothing as they both clicked their seatbelts into place and he started the powerful machine with a seductive purr.

But when she saw that they weren't heading for his home in Dalkeith—was that what she'd secretly been hoping for?—but for the centre of the city, she turned to look at his harsh profile.

'Where are you taking me?' she demanded.

'I'm taking you——' he changed gear with a soft expletive as a truck careered in front of them '—to see someone I visited last week.'

'What the...?' But her words died away when she saw that he'd screeched to a halt in front of Caro's Kitchen Cookies, and seconds later he was round at her side of the car, had unclipped her seatbelt and was pulling her out.

He just wouldn't let go of her, even as he pushed the door of the office open. *Damn* but it was infuriating how she responded just to that innocent clasping of hands. His touch brought memories flooding back...

'What the hell do you think you're *doing*?' she spat. Surely he wasn't planning to confront Caro?

He was.

With a set, determined look on his face he marched straight into Caro's office, where the air was thick with the smell of cheroots. Caro, dressed from head to toe in scarlet, was reading a book on yoga and munching away at a corned-beef sandwich. She looked up as they entered.

'Hello, dear,' she said mildly to Kitty, then her face lit up. 'Mr Spielberg!' she exclaimed.

Darius sighed. 'Miss Peters, as I told you last week, I am *not* Steven Spielberg. My name is Darius Speed.'

'Oh, yes,' she giggled.

He towered over the desk. 'Kitty here is under the impression that I'm planning to use a film-script that you sent me *under my own name*.'

Caro blinked. 'Well, you are, aren't you?'

'I have never,' Darius thundered, '*ever* seen a film-script purporting to come from you!'

There was a momentary pause.

Caro lifted her eyes to stare at Darius. 'Oh, dear—then I must have sent it to Mr Spielberg.'

Darius's mouth twitched in a smile. 'You actually sent a film-script to Steven Spielberg?'

Caro shrugged. 'Well, not actually the *whole* script. I just jotted down a couple of ideas I'd had. Asked him to drop in to see me to discuss them next time he was visiting Oz.'

'But you told me that Darius had taken it!' exploded Kitty.

Caro blinked. 'Did I, dear?'

Kitty didn't know whether to laugh or cry. Or both. She turned and ran out of the office, but Darius was hot on her heels.

He grabbed hold of her arm, but she shook it off.

'Go away!' she shouted.

She ran off again, but he kept up with her easily, seemingly oblivious to the stares they were attracting, and it wasn't until she was completely out of breath that she stopped and faced him.

His own breath came as steadily as if he'd simply been for a gentle stroll. The man had stamina, she'd say that for him.

'Going to talk now?' he said calmly.

And the man had cheek! 'Listen to me!' she cried. 'This changes nothing, don't you see? You still mistrusted me, still set me up——'

'No, you listen to me!' he said harshly. 'But not here. I don't intend to have a show-down with you in the middle of the street!'

He lifted an arm to hail a cab, and one materialised instantly. He directed the driver to take them to the Swan River and didn't say another word until he had steered her to a bench and they were seated, dazzled by the rippling refractions of light on the water.

'You talk about mistrust, Kitty,' he said quietly, 'but you didn't trust me either——'

'At first I didn't!' she interrupted hotly.

'But then you got to know me and decided you were wrong,' he put in. 'Didn't you?'

'And then you set me up!' she said bitterly. 'After you'd made love to me.'

'I was in the same boat as you,' he said quietly. 'If it's a matter of trust we're talking about, we were both suspicious, circling round each other like wary animals, and occasionally we'd collide and then—wham!—spontaneous combustion. Common sense told me to get rid of you early on—the trouble was that I fancied you like mad.' He smiled. 'Then, as I got to know you better, my judgement of you underwent a dramatic change, and all my suspicious thoughts flew straight out of my head.

'But there was still something niggling—an area of constraint coming from you which I couldn't work out. I tried to get you to tell me—do you remember the truth game we played?—but you wouldn't.

'And then I made love to you—because no power on earth could have stopped me. But there was still that barrier between us. Simon had told me that you'd asked him questions about the safe so, yes, I guess I left the script out as a last measure—the dangled carrot. The trouble was that when I came back and caught you red-handed I completely lost my cool. I said a lot of things I shouldn't have, and I'm sorry.'

He sighed. 'After you'd gone and I'd had a chance to think about it, it occurred to me that you'd been persuaded to rob me because of your sweet, generous and trusting nature. So I went to see Caro and I realised that she's kind and well-intentioned—but as nutty as a fruit-cake.'

She saw the glimmer in his eyes and bit her lip to hide her smile. 'Steven Spielberg!' she said. 'Oh, Darius—I've been so stupid. How could I have been taken in by something like that?'

'You haven't been stupid,' he contradicted her. 'You've been beautiful and crazy and gorgeous— I've been the stupid one. Now come here and kiss me.' He drew her into his arms, but he didn't kiss her then; he was too busy scowling. 'Were you really going out this afternoon with that chef?' he demanded.

She felt a little thrill that he could look so absolutely furious. She decided to put him out of his misery. 'No,' she admitted, and parted her lips expectantly.

Still nothing. His gaze had grown even more intense. 'Why did you let me take your virginity, Kitty?' he asked in a strangely husky voice.

Her heart was beating furiously. Because I love you, you idiot! Why else? 'Because I thought I was frigid,' she lied.

'Frigid?' He laughed softly. 'Really? What kind of insensitive fool told you that?' And as he slowly moved his tongue inside her mouth Hugo and his blustering lies were consigned to history.

Heat flooded through her as his arms went round her shoulders, and she was filled with an unbearably strong impulse to tip her head back, to receive his kiss and give it back to him in full. But what was the point? Wouldn't she just get more and more hurt? She should push him away, get up. Something. But with him kissing her like that it was hard to do anything but let him ...

'I've missed you, Kitty,' he whispered. 'Have you missed me too?'

Yes, oh, yes.

'Have you?'

Desperately, but she wasn't going to tell him *that*. 'A little,' she whispered, and heard him laugh softly before his mouth came back down on hers to inflict more of the same sweet and powerful drug.

'Let's go home,' he said roughly.

Home? Her eyes fluttered open in confusion as she came back to the present, the tingling in her breasts making coherent thought almost impossible. 'You mean—you want me to come back to work for you?'

He gave a lazy laugh, his eyes shining silver like the sheen of a sword-blade. 'Why don't we put your employment on a far more casual footing?' he murmured. 'Why don't you come and live with me?'

Kitty stared at the face before her, at the silvery light which shone in his eyes.

'Live with you?' she repeated.

'Why not? That's what people in this situation usually do, isn't it?'

'In this situation'? He made it sound like a treatise he was submitting. 'What situation?' she asked.

'Having a relationship,' he drawled in a mock-American accent as he picked up her hand and kissed the palm.

'Are we? Having a relationship?' She jokily mimicked his accent.

'Mmm.' His tongue traced a line from the fleshy pad of her palm to her left ring-finger. 'I rather think we are. And I rather think I'd like you in my bed every night, Miss Goodman. And most afternoons.'

'I've never lived with anyone before, Darius.'

'I'm hardly the seasoned professional myself,' he murmured.

So what did that mean? she wondered. That he *had* lived with someone, or that he hadn't? 'I'm not sure I'll be any good at it.'

'It's easy,' he murmured. 'And with you it'll be like taking candy from a baby...'

She let her head sink down on to his shoulder, glad and sad at the same time. She supposed that this was the modern way. People lived together first.

First? Surely she wasn't crazily thinking that this was a trial marriage? He'd made no mention of

love or marriage. And why should he? Loads of
people didn't bother getting married these days;
they had 'relationships' instead. There was even a
name for it. Serial monogamy, that was it. Far more
sensible than talking about 'love' and then con-
tributing to the divorce-rate. It was true that once
upon a time she had somehow imagined herself
drifting down the aisle in a cloud of white organza,
but that was when she'd been imagining being
married to Mr Ordinary. And Darius was no Mr
Ordinary.

He pulled her to her feet and began to kiss her
again, and the kiss drove all sense and doubts from
her mind.

Somehow they found their way back to the car
and she suspected that he exceeded the speed-limit
several times on the way back to his house. It all
seemed like a very unreal dream until he undressed
her, kissed her tenderly and told her she was
beautiful—which she didn't believe—then drove her
to fulfilment, before spilling his seed inside her
while she said a little prayer that the contraception
they were using would fail.

Yes, it was all perfect except for one thing.

She wanted to tell him she loved him very much.

But, being a cool, modern woman, she couldn't.

CHAPTER THIRTEEN

'YOU'RE getting very good at that,' said Darius eventually, lying back against the pillow and stroking the rumpled red hair which lay fanned across his chest.

'Am I?'

'Mmm.' He smiled. 'You know you are. And to think that it was your innocence that appealed to me!'

'Seducer!'

'Temptress!'

'Darius...'

'Mmm?' he said sleepily.

What was this compulsion that made some women, like her, stray into areas which were best left ignored? 'Did you live with anyone—before me?' Kitty made two fingers walk down his torso to rest in the indentation of his navel.

There was a moment's silence, while she sensed his mental retreat.

'No,' he said shortly.

'But there must have been someone serious.'

'Once. A long time ago. Now leave it, Kitty— I don't want to talk about it.' He cradled her against him, spoon-fashion, and even before she felt his breathing become long and steady she knew that he was falling asleep.

She stored this new piece of information in her head, where it lay uncomfortably, as a heavy meal sometimes lay on the stomach. So there *had* been someone. She wondered why he didn't want to talk about her. Perhaps Simon knew about the girl in his past.

She felt the scrape of his chin against her back. He had brought her to bed after lunch, and had spent the next three hours making love to her. *Three hours*! The man was the most perfect lover she could imagine and, to her delight, her own eagerness to be taught seemed to thrill him equally. And sometimes, when she was in his arms, he treated her with such exquisite tenderness that it was easy to fool herself that he was a little bit in love with her.

If only...

Still, if she couldn't have that, she had everything but. Over the next few days she found that it was surprisingly easy to live together as man and wife—no, as man and woman, she corrected herself fiercely. Perhaps not so very surprising considering that she loved him so much that sometimes she thought she might explode with it.

She loved the way he introduced her now as his girlfriend, in that deep, rich voice of his. Or the way his eyes met and mocked her if he was working at a crowded table on his script, sending a secret, sensual message for her eyes only. Every opportunity they had, they would sail together to Rottnest—Darius was teaching her to crew—and they would spend hours walking over the sea-soaked sand, hand in hand, talking, talking, talking. She'd never been to university, never sat and had long, late-night dissections of life and soul, and yet now she had it all with Darius. He, it seemed, never tired of questioning things. She suspected that was what made his films so challenging.

She couldn't feel anything other than affectionate humour towards Caro, and she didn't dwell on the fact that things could have turned out very differently. Darius even dropped Caro a note saying that if she ever *completed* a film-script then he'd be happy to look at it.

One other piece of good news was that Brent Salisbury's wife was suddenly and unexpectedly pregnant again—with twins. She needed live-in help; they had a very large property, and Darius recommended Wayne's mother. Shortly afterwards, the two of them, plus Mersey the cat, were happily living in a nice-sized cottage on the Salisbury estate, much to the chagrin of Anna-Maria Rawlings!

So one week slipped slowly into two, three, then a month. Even Simon seemed to approve of the changed living arrangements.

'I've never seen Darius looking so happy,' he remarked one day, coming into the kitchen and watching as Kitty made brown-bread ice-cream for the next day's lunch. 'He needed a woman to domesticate him.'

Well, hardly that. 'Domesticated' wasn't really a word which rode well on Darius's shoulders. He might be worldly, urbane and sophisticated on the outside . . . but inside was a kind of dark, elemental

streak. He showed that side in bed. In bed he was
no gentleman . . .

Kitty shivered with erotic memory, even though
the hot Australian sun blazed in through the
window. 'Simon,' she said suddenly, 'can I ask you
something?'

That night Kitty's mother rang, and as she quietly
replaced the receiver Kitty looked up to find Darius
staring at her, his brows narrowed.

'Homesick?' he queried.

'Not really.'

'Not even a bit?'

She smiled. 'Perhaps just a *bit*.'

'We could,' he suggested casually, 'take a trip to
England—if you'd like to see your mother.'

Her eyes widened. 'Together?'

'Sure.'

She had a sudden and vivid impression of Darius,
all tousled dark hair and long limbs and disturbingly good looks, sitting in the pristine elegance of
her mother's drawing-room. Her mother, who regarded men generally as the enemy, whose idea of
suitable husband material had been Hugo—how
would she react to the overwhelmingly sensual and
physical Darius?

And you aren't married! mocked a small voice.
That's really the reason why you don't want to take
him. Even when you know that it's wrong—that
your mother shouldn't have any influence on how
you live your life.

But it wasn't always as easy as that. To some
extent she had always lived in her mother's shadow.

Twenty-four years of not very subtle indoctrination on how shocking it was that people no longer cared about the sanctity of marriage—well, those twenty-four years didn't just disappear overnight.

Kitty swallowed. 'I'm not that fussed about going. Honestly.'

Silver eyes had narrowed into discerning slivers of frosted metal. 'Your mother's fairly conventional, right?'

'You could say that.'

'Tell me about her.'

He was so direct sometimes. She'd grown up in an environment where being direct was anathema. But Darius had a way of asking a question, a way of looking at you as he asked it, which made you want to pour your heart out to him.

'She was brought up that way. Never show your feelings. Stiff upper lip and all that.' She laughed. 'Her idea of the worst crime you could commit would be eating in the street!'

'So what would be her objection to me? That as a film director I'm deemed unconventional?'

'No.' She shook her head. 'She respects money— and you've certainly got enough of that.'

'That we're not married, then?'

Kitty flushed to the roots of her hair and turned away. 'Of course not.'

But he was on his feet and beside her, turning her to face him, his voice almost gentle. 'Kitty?'

'Oh, for goodness' sake—I'm not holding you to ransom to marry me just because my mother wouldn't approve of us living in sin!'

Grey eyes crinkled just very slightly at the corners. 'My, my, Kitty—emotive words indeed.'

She could have groaned aloud. Living in sin, indeed! What modern woman would ever use such an outdated line? It made her sound as though she were fresh out of the convent!

He picked up one of her hands, turned it over as he often did, rubbing each freckle with his forefinger. When he looked up, his face was almost stern. 'Well, let's get married, then, shall we?'

It should have been the answer to all her dreams. She should have flung herself into his arms, swooning, and accepted on the spot. Instead, she gave a watery smile, meaning to say yes, but it didn't happen quite like that and she burst into noisy tears.

He tried to gather her into his arms, but her fists went out to drum away, uselessly, at the solid wall of his chest.

'My, my,' he murmured. 'Not quite the reception a man hopes for when he proposes.' And without another word he picked Kitty up and flung her, still kicking and punching ineffectually, over his shoulder and strode out towards the staircase.

'Put me down!' she wailed. Then, 'Where are you taking me?'

'The only place where I can be sure of submission.' But the laughter in his voice mocked his words.

'The—bedroom?' She wavered, her heart beating like a piston as the door loomed up in front of them and he kicked it open.

'Right first time. Because when big girls have tantrums they get treated like——' she landed in a soft heap in the centre of the bed '—little girls. Now——' and he lay down on top of her, his elbows taking his weight, his face, darkly intense, just inches away from her '—tell me why you reacted like that just now when I asked you to marry me. I thought you'd like me to make an honest woman of you.'

She shook her head from side to side, aware of how frightful she must look with her tear-stained and blotchy face, knowing that, any minute now, all her insecurities would come bubbling to the surface in a great molten mass. 'I certainly don't want you to marry me because you think my mother would prefer it——'

'Your mother has nothing to do with it.'

'And I certainly don't want you marrying me out of pity!'

He frowned. 'I'm not with you.'

'*Pity*! P-I-T-Y! Because you feel sorry for me.'

'Kitty, I don't believe that in the history of the world any man would have married a woman because he felt sorry for her.'

She squirmed underneath him, but when she saw his appreciative smile she realised that she was having entirely the wrong effect and stopped. 'It was the most lukewarm and half-hearted proposal I've ever heard——'

'That's because my mouth was very dry,' he commented.

She stared at him suspiciously. 'Don't try and tell me you were nervous,' she accused.

'Why not? Aren't I allowed to be nervous? It isn't every day that I ask a woman to marry me!'

This set her off again. 'Obviously not, or you might have told me you loved me—even if you *were* lying through your teeth.'

He had gone very still. 'Is that what all this is about, Kitty?' he asked quietly. 'Love?'

Now she was in full flow. 'I know how much you loved your girlfriend at college. I know how beautiful she was. I know that you couldn't possibly feel the same way about me—but you might at least *pretend*...' Oh, lord. Now she sounded like a desperado.

'Shh, Kitty,' he soothed. 'Stop crying.' He brushed her tears away with the back of his hand. 'Who told you about Pamela?'

'Simon did. But only because I asked—you see, you never talk about her, Darius. He said how devastated you were when she died.'

'I was,' he said quietly. 'She was only nineteen.'

Her eyes shimmered, and she felt suddenly ashamed of herself for resurrecting his grief. If she couldn't cope with the fact that he had loved someone else, then that was her problem. She should put up or shut up. 'I shouldn't have brought it up; it was——'

'We met at college,' he interrupted her, and smoothed a curl off her forehead. 'It was over ten years ago, and, yes, I loved Pamela—in the way a twenty-one-year-old on the threshold of manhood loves a girl. It was the heady but unreal buzz of first love—we didn't even live together—and it probably would have fizzled out naturally had Pamela not...' His silver eyes met hers in a steady, sad stare. 'Pam was two years behind me, and I had just left college. I'd got my first big break and was working on a commercial in Canberra. Pamela's sister was having a big birthday party and Pam wanted me to go, but...' He hesitated. 'I told her no—said I was too busy. That my work was important. She slammed the phone down on me. Next morning she was dead.'

Kitty blanched at the stark note in his voice. '*How*?' she whispered.

'She'd gone to the party, and accepted a lift home from some lunatic on a motorcycle. They'd hit a tree at eighty miles an hour. They were killed instantly.' His voice hardened. 'And I never forgave myself for not being there when she needed me. If I'd been there, she might still be alive today.'

'But you couldn't have foreseen that that would happen,' she protested. 'How could you?'

'But feelings aren't always rational, are they, Kitty? Which is why I'm kind of superstitious about the word "love". My father may have been a workshy parasite whom I sometimes despised for the way he treated my mother—but that didn't stop me loving him. And when he died perhaps my grief was compounded by the fact that at times I *had* despised him. Then my mother died.' His eyes shuttered to conceal the sudden, terrifying bleakness. 'Then Pamela... You see, Kitty, in my world it always seemed that the people I loved would be taken from me—and I couldn't take that risk with you.' His voice softened as he looked down at her. 'Don't you know how much I love you, my darling?'

Her eyes widened and her mouth trembled. 'Honestly? Truly?'

He smiled. 'Honestly. Truly. And I rather thought that you loved me too.'

'Oh, Darius, I *do*. Really I do—so much.'

'But you never said.'

'Even modern women have their pride,' she answered primly. 'And it *is* customary for the man to declare himself first.'

'You? *Modern*?' He threw his head back and laughed. 'Kitty, you're as old-fashioned as applepie.'

Apprehension reared its ugly head. She thought of the countless women there must have been over the years—women whose physical perfection the silver screen magnified. 'I can be modern,' she whispered. 'I want to be.'

'Rubbish. I don't want a woman like that.' He brought her hand up to his mouth and kissed it. 'Sure, I've done the jet-set life, the nightclub scene—but I'd had it with all that long ago. I've waited all my life for someone like you—someone who will love me, and fill my house with children and animals, the smell of baking filling the air.'

She heard the wistful tone in his voice as he described the childhood he should have had himself, and she made a silent vow to Mrs Speed, wherever she was, that she would love and cherish her son.

'But what about your films?' she questioned. 'Won't you need to travel for those?' And wouldn't she, however much he told her he loved her, worry about the beautiful actresses who would inevitably fling themselves at him?

He shook his head and grinned. 'I've touched home base. I want to stay here. With you. Or we can travel—*together*. I want you with me, Kitty, not away from me. You can style my films for me——'

'That's nepotism!' she protested.

'No, it's not. My instincts tell me you'd be very good indeed. Or you could write a cookery-book—yes, of course you could! And fortunately I've invested enough money in property and business that I don't actually *need* to work for the money. I can concentrate on filming here in Oz—fan the flames of our home-grown film industry even more. Kitty——' he frowned. '—what's wrong? Why are you looking at me like that?'

If she didn't tell him, she'd never be free of the fear. 'There must have been hundreds of women in your past, yet you never talk about them.'

'Not hundreds,' he corrected her gently. 'A few. And the reason I don't talk about them is because they aren't important. They never were, really, not compared with what I feel about you. I can't erase my past, Kitty, but it's of no consequence. I had to wait a long time for you. You were lucky,' he grinned. 'You found me first time around!'

But she still had to voice the dark fear. She cleared her throat. 'It's just that—well, you could have—anyone, really—and yet you want me. And I'm not beautiful——'

'Yes, you are,' he contradicted her softly. 'The most beautiful woman I've ever met. *Yes*!' He framed her face with two reverent palms, bent his head to whisper a kiss of delectable sweetness on to her trembling lips. 'So when——' he kissed her again '—are we getting married?'

She gave the contented smile of the cat who had not only got the cream, but the entire contents of the jug. 'I haven't said yes yet. And aren't you supposed to get down on one knee to propose?' she teased.

'Mmm. Perhaps.' He bent his head to nuzzle her ear. 'But I can think of a much more satisfactory position, can't you?'

She wrapped her arms tightly around his back. She most certainly could!

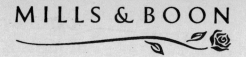

MILLS & BOON

Next Month's Romances

Each month you can choose from a wide variety of romance with Mills & Boon. Below are the new titles to look out for next month.

IN NEED OF A WIFE	Emma Darcy
PRINCE OF LIES	Robyn Donald
THE ONE AND ONLY	Carole Mortimer
CHRIS	Sally Wentworth
TO CATCH A PLAYBOY	Elizabeth Duke
DANGEROUS DECEIVER	Lindsay Armstrong
PROMISE OF PASSION	Natalie Fox
DARK PIRATE	Angela Devine
HEARTLESS PURSUIT	Jessica Steele
PLAYING FOR KEEPS	Rosemary Hammond
BLIND OBSESSION	Lee Wilkinson
THE RANCHER AND THE REDHEAD	
	Rebecca Winters
WHO'S HOLDING THE BABY?	Day Leclaire
THE BARBARIAN'S BRIDE	Alex Ryder
SLEEPING BEAUTY	Jane Donnelly
THE REAL McCOY	Patricia Knoll

Available from WH Smith, John Menzies, Volume One, Forbuoys, Martins, Woolworths, Tesco, Asda, Safeway and other paperback stockists.

A years supply of Mills & Boon romances — absolutely free!

Would you like to win a years supply of heartwarming and passionate romances? Well, you can and they're FREE! All you have to do is complete the word puzzle below and send it to us by 29th February 1996. The first 5 correct entries picked out of the bag after that date will win a years supply of Mills & Boon romances (six books every month—worth over £100). What could be easier?

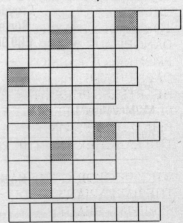

GMWIMSIN

✂ NNSAUT

ACEHB

EMSMUR

ANCOE

DNSA

RTOISTU

THEOL

ATYCH

NSU

MYSTERY DESTINATION

Please turn over for details on how to enter

How to enter

Simply sort out the jumbled letters to make ten words all to do with being on holiday. Enter your answers in the grid, then unscramble the letters in the shaded squares to find out our mystery holiday destination.

After you have completed the word puzzle and found our mystery destination, don't forget to fill in your name and address in the space provided below and return this page in an envelope (you don't need a stamp). Competition ends 29th February 1996.

Mills & Boon Romance Holiday Competition
FREEPOST
P.O. Box 344
Croydon
Surrey
CR9 9EL

Are you a Reader Service Subscriber?   Yes ❏   No ❏

Ms/Mrs/Miss/Mr _____

Address _____

_____

_____ Postcode _____

One application per household.

You may be mailed with other offers from other reputable companies as a result of this application. If you would prefer not to receive such offers, please tick box. ❏

mps
MAILING
PREFERENCE
SERVICE

COMP495
B